Please return / renew by date shown.
You can renew it at:
norlink.norfolk.gov.uk
or by telephone: 0344 800 8006
Please have your library card & PIN ready

USA TODAY bestselling author **Lynn Raye Harris** burst onto the scene when she won a writing contest held by Mills & Boon®. The prize was a ~~a year~~—but only six months later Lynn sold her first novel. A former finalist for the Romance Writers of America's Golden Heart Award, Lynn lives in Alabama with her handsome husband and two crazy cats. Her stories have been called 'exceptional and emotional', 'intense', and 'sizzling'. You can visit her at www.lynnrayeharris.com

Recent titles by the same author:

Did you know these are also available as eBooks?
Visit www.millsandboon.co.uk

THE CHANGE IN DI NAVARRA'S PLAN

BY
LYNN RAYE HARRIS

First published in Great Britain 2013
by Mills & Boon, an imprint of Harlequin (UK) Limited,
Harlequin (UK) Limited, Eton House, 18-24 Paradise Road,
Richmond, Surrey TW9 1SR

© Lynn Raye Harris 2013

ISBN: 978 0 263 90069 9

Harlequin (UK) policy is to use papers that are natural, renewable and recyclable products and made from wood grown in sustainable forests. The logging and manufacturing process conform to the legal environmental regulations of the country of origin.

Printed and bound in Spain
by Blackprint CPI, Barcelona

THE CHANGE IN
DI NAVARRA'S
PLAN

One more time for my sweet cat, Miss Pitty Pat (MPP). This is the last book we wrote together before she succumbed to heart disease. Which, of course, means I wrote it and she lay on my feet or legs or lap, depending on her mood. I miss her like crazy.

CHAPTER ONE

"YOU, GET UP."

Holly Craig looked up at the man standing so tall and imposing before her. Her heart skipped a beat at the sheer masculine beauty of his face. He had dark hair, piercing gray eyes and a jaw that had been chiseled out of Carrara marble. His nose was elegant, tapered, and his cheekbones were so pretty that supermodels must surely swoon in envy at the sight.

"Come on, girl, I don't have all day," he said, his tones sophisticated and clipped. And Italian, she realized. He had an accent that wasn't thick. Rather, it was refined and smooth, like fine wine. Or fine perfume.

Holly clutched her case—a secondhand case that wasn't even real leather—to her chest and shifted on the couch. "I—I'm not sure you have the right—"

He snapped his fingers. "You are here to see me, yes?"

Holly swallowed. "You are Mr. Di Navarra?"

He looked irritated. "Indeed."

Holly jumped up, her heart thrumming a quick tempo. Her skin flushed with embarrassment. She should have known this man was the powerful head of Navarra Cosmetics. It wasn't as if she'd never seen a photo of the man who might just hold her entire future in his hands. Everyone knew who Drago di Navarra was.

Everyone except her, it would seem. This meeting was

so important, and already she'd got off on the wrong foot. *Easy, ma belle,* her grandmother would have said. *You can do this.*

Holly stuck her hand out. "Mr. Di Navarra, yes, I'm Holly—"

He waved a hand, cutting her off. "Who you are isn't important." His gaze narrowed, dropped down over her. She'd worn her best suit today, but it was at least five years out of season. Still, it was black and serviceable. And it was all she had. She lifted her chin, confused by the strange meeting thus far, but not yet willing to ruin it by calling him on his rudeness.

"Turn around," he ordered.

Holly's cheeks flamed. But she did it, slowly turning in a circle until she faced him again.

"Yes," he said to an assistant who hovered nearby. "I think this one will do. Let them know we're coming."

"Yes, sir," the woman said, her manner cool and efficient as she turned and strode back toward the office they'd both emerged from.

"Let's go," Drago said. Holly could only stand and watch him stride away from her, bewilderment muddling her head and gluing her feet to the floor.

He seemed to realize she wasn't with him, because he stopped and turned around. He looked impatient rather than angry, though she suspected angry was next on the agenda.

"Are you coming or not?"

Holly had a choice. She could say no, she wasn't coming. She could tell him he was rude and appalling and she'd come here for an appointment, and not to be talked down to, scrutinized and ordered around.

Or she could go, figure out what his strange manner was all about and get her chance to pitch him her ideas. The case in her hands was warm, fragrant with the samples she'd tucked inside. It reminded her of home, of her grand-mother and the many hours they'd spent together dreaming about taking their perfumes to the next level, instead of only blending them for the friends and townspeople who purchased their custom combinations.

She'd come a long way to see this man. She'd spent every bit of savings she had getting here, with only enough for her lodging and the return trip home again. If she lost this opportunity, she lost far more than money. She lost her dream. She lost Gran's dream. She'd have to go home and start over again.

Because Gran was dead and the house would soon be gone. She couldn't afford to keep it any longer. Unless she convinced Drago di Navarra that she had something worth investing in. Something worth taking a chance on.

And she would do whatever it took to get that opportunity.

"Yes," she said firmly. "I'm coming."

Drago could feel her eyes upon him. It was nothing he wasn't accustomed to. Women often stared. It was not something he felt was an inconvenience. No, it was an advantage, especially for a man in the business he was in.

In the business of making people more beautiful, it did not hurt to be attractive yourself. If much of that was genetics, well, it was not his fault.

He still used Navarra products—soap, cologne, skin care, shampoo—and he would always maintain, to who-ever would listen, that they benefited him greatly.

Now he sat in the back of the limousine with his projec-tions and printouts, and studied the focus-group informa-tion for the newest line of products NC was bringing out this fall. He was pleased with what he saw. Very pleased.

He was not, it should be noted, pleased with the agency that had sent this girl over. She was the fourth model he'd seen this morning, and though they'd finally got it right, he was angry that it had taken four attempts to get the correct combination of innocence and sex appeal that he'd desired for this ad campaign.

He was selling freshness and beauty, not a prepackaged look that many of the models he'd seen recently came with. They had a hard edge about them, something that looked out from their eyes and said that, while they might appear innocent, they had actually left innocence in the rearview mirror a thousand miles ago.

This girl, however...

He looked up, met her gaze boldly, appraisingly. She dropped her eyes quickly, a pink stain spreading over her cheeks. A sharp feeling knifed into him, stunning him. He had a visceral reaction to that display of sweetness, his body hardening in a way it hadn't in quite some time. Oh, he'd had sex—plenty of it—but it had become more of a box to check off in his day rather than an escape or a way to relax.

His reaction just now interested him. His gaze slipped over her again, appraised what he saw, as he had the first time. She was dressed in a cheap suit, though it fit her well. Her shoes were tall, pink suede—and brand-new, he realized, looking at the sole of one where she'd turned her legs to the side. The price tag was still on the shoe. He tilted his head.

$49.99

Not Jimmy Choo shoes or Manolo Blahnik shoes, certainly. He didn't expect her to be wearing thousand-dollar shoes, or even the latest designer fashions, but he had rather expected she would be more...polished.

Which was odd, considering that polish was precisely what he did not want. Still, she was a model with a highly respected New York City firm. He'd have thought she might be a bit more prepared. On the other hand, perhaps she was fresh from the farm and they'd sent her over straightaway in desperation.

"How many of these jobs have you done before?" he asked.

She looked up again. Blinked. Her eyes were blue. Her hair was the most extraordinary shade of strawberry-blond, and a smattering of light freckles dotted her pale skin. He would have to tell the photographer not to erase those later. They added to her fresh look.

"Jobs?"

Drago suppressed a stab of impatience. "Modeling jobs, *cara*."

She blinked again. "Oh, I, um…"

"I'm not going to send you away if this is your first time," he snapped. "So long as the camera loves you, I couldn't care less if you've just come up from the family farm."

Her skin flushed again. This time, her chin came up. Her eyes flashed cool fire, and he found himself intrigued at the play of emotions across her face. It was almost as if she were arguing with herself.

"There's no need to be rude, you know," she snapped back. "Manners are still important, whether you've got a billion dollars or only one."

Drago had a sudden urge to laugh. It was as if a kitten had suddenly hissed and swatted him. And it had the effect of making some of his tension drain away.

"Then I apologize for being rude," he said, amused.

She folded her arms over her breasts and tried to look stern. "Well, then. Thank you."

He set the papers down on the seat beside him. "Is this your first time to New York?"

Her tongue darted out to moisten her lower lip. A slice of sensation knifed into his groin. "Yes," she said.

"And where are you from?"

"Louisiana."

He leaned forward then, suddenly quite certain he needed to make her feel comfortable if he was going to get what he wanted out of this shoot. "You'll do a fine job," he said. "Just be yourself in front of the camera. Don't try to act glamorous."

She dropped her gaze away and slid her fingers along the hem of her jacket. "Mr. Di Navarra—"

"Drago," he said.

She looked up again. Her blue eyes were worried. He had a sudden urge to kiss her, to wipe away that worried look and put a different kind of look there. He gave himself a mental shake. Highly uncharacteristic of him. Not that he didn't date the models—he did sometimes—but this one wasn't his usual type. He liked the tall, elegant ones. The ones who looked as if ice cubes wouldn't melt in their mouths.

The ones who didn't make him think of wide-eyed idealists who chased after dreams—and kept chasing them even when they led down self-destructive paths. Women like this one were so easily corruptible in the wrong hands. His protective instincts came to the fore, made him want to send her back to Louisiana before she even stepped in front of the camera.

He wanted her to go home, to stop chasing after New York dreams of fame and fortune. This world would only disappoint her. In a few months, she'd be shooting drugs, drinking alcohol and throwing up her food in order to lose that extra pound some idiotic industry type had told her made her look fat.

Before he could say anything of what he was thinking, the car came to a halt. The door swung open immediately. "Sir, thank goodness," the location manager said. "The girl isn't here and—"

"I have her," Drago said. The other man's head swung

around until his gaze landed on the girl—Holly, was it? Now he wished he'd paid more attention when he'd first seen her outside his office.

"Excellent." The man wiggled his fingers at her. "Come along, then. Let's get you into makeup."

She looked terrified. Drago smiled encouragingly. "Go, Holly," he said, trying the name he was fairly certain was correct. He didn't miss the slight widening of her eyes, and knew he'd got it right. Clearly, she hadn't expected him to remember. "I will see you again when this is over."

She looked almost relieved as her eyes darted between him and the location manager. "Y-you will?"

She seemed very alone in that moment. Something inside him rose to the fore, made him ask a question he knew he shouldn't. "Are you busy for dinner?"

She shook her head.

Drago smiled. He shouldn't do this, he knew it, and yet he was going to anyway. "Then consider yourself busy now."

Holly had never been to a fancy restaurant in her life, but she was in one now—in a private room, no less—sitting across from a man who might just be the most handsome man she'd ever seen in her life. The longer she spent in Drago di Navarra's company, the more fascinated she was.

Oh, he hadn't started out well, that was for sure—but he'd improved tremendously upon further acquaintance. He'd actually turned out to be…nice.

There was only one problem. Holly frowned as she listened to him talk about the photo shoot earlier. She wasn't a model, but she'd stood there in Central Park and let people fuss over her, dress her in a flowing purple gown, paint her with makeup, tease her hair—and then she'd stepped in front of the camera and froze, wondering how she'd let this thing go so far.

She'd only wanted a chance to tell Drago di Navarra about her perfumes, but she hadn't known where they were going or what he expected until it was too late. She'd choked when she should have explained. But she'd been worried that if she explained who she was and what she wanted, he would be angry with her.

And that wasn't going to work, was it?

Still, as she'd stood there, frozen, she'd known it was over. Her dream was dead, because she was going to have to explain to all these people watching her that she truly had no idea what she was doing.

But then Drago had walked onto the shoot and smiled at her. She'd smiled back, and suddenly the photographer was happy. She was certain she'd still been awkward and out of place, but everyone had seemed delighted with her. They'd changed her clothes, her hair, her makeup several times. And she'd stood in front of that camera, thinking of her perfumes and wondering how on earth she was going to explain herself to Drago, until someone finally told her they were done.

Then Drago had whisked her off for dinner and she'd clammed up like a frightened schoolgirl. She was still wearing the last dress they'd put on her, a pretty, silky sheath in eggplant and a pair of gold Christian Louboutin pumps. This entire experience was a fantasy come to life in many ways. She was in New York City, being wined and dined by one of the most eligible bachelors in the world, and she wanted to remember every moment of it.

And yet everything about this day was wrong, because she'd come here to pitch her perfume, not model for Navarra Cosmetics. How could she tell him? How could she find the perfect moment to say "Oh, Drago, thank you for the dinner, but what I really want to talk to you about is my perfume"?

Still, she had to. And soon. But every time she tried to

open her mouth and tell him, something stopped her. There were interruptions, distractions. When he reached across the table and took her hand in his, every last thought in her head flew out the window.

"You were fabulous today, Holly," he said. And then he lifted her hand to his lips and pressed them against the back of her hand. A sizzle of electricity shot through her, gathered in her feminine core and made her ache in ways she'd never quite experienced before.

She'd had a boyfriend back home. She'd been kissed. They'd even gone further than that—but she'd never felt the moment was right to go all the way.

And then he'd broken up with her. Taken up with that catty Lisa Tate instead. It still stung.

You're too selfish, Holly, he'd said. *Too focused on your damn perfume.*

Yes, she was focused. Holly dragged herself back to the present, tried so hard to ignore the skittering of her pulse and the throbbing deep in her core. She knew what this was. She might not have had sex before, but she wasn't stupid. She'd experienced desire with Colin, but she'd just never got to the point where she'd tumbled over the edge into hedonism.

She could imagine it with this man. Her heart skipped as she met Drago di Navarra's smoky gray eyes. *Tell him, Holly. Tell him now....*

"Thank you," she said, dropping her gaze from the intensity of his as her pulse shot forward again.

"You're quite a natural. I predict you will go far in this business if you don't allow yourself to be corrupted by it."

She opened her mouth to speak, but his cell phone rang. He glanced down at the display, and then said something in Italian that could have been a curse.

"You must excuse me," he said, picking up the phone. "This is important."

"Of course," she replied, but he'd already answered the call. She sat with her hands in her lap and waited for him to finish.

Holly gazed at the silk wallpaper and the gilt fixtures, and felt as if she'd landed on another planet. What was she doing here? How had she ended up in the company of a billionaire, having dinner with him as if it were a daily occurrence?

Everything about her trip to New York thus far was so different from her usual experience that she could hardly get her bearings.

Why couldn't she seem to say what she needed to say? She'd feel better if she had her samples. With those, she could find her way through this strange landscape. But her samples were in her case, which was stowed in his car. That had given her pause, but he'd convinced her that her belongings would be fine while they ate dinner.

If only she had her case, she could open it up and pull out her samples. She could explain her concepts, sell him on the beauty of Colette, the last perfume she and her grandmother had worked on together. It was the best one, though her ideas for others were infinite. She got a tingle of excitement just thinking about the blend of smooth essences, water and alcohol that produced the final product.

Drago finished his call and apologized for the interruption. "Forgive me, *bella mia*," he said. "But the beauty industry never sleeps."

"It's fine," she told him, smiling. Her heart was beating fast again, but she'd finally settled on a plan of action. Once she was reunited with her case, she would explain to this man why she was really here. She was certain he couldn't say no once she'd given him a whiff of Colette.

Their dinner came then, and Holly found herself relaxing in Drago's company. He was completely charming. He was attentive, sending most of his calls to voice mail, and interested in what she had to say.

She told him about Louisiana, about her grandmother—without mentioning perfume, since that had to wait for her samples—and about the trip to New York on the bus.

He blinked. "You came all this way on a bus?"

Holly dropped her gaze to her plate as heat seared her cheeks. "I couldn't afford to fly," she said. But she had spent nearly everything she had scraping together the money for this brief trip. Just to talk to this man, for pity's sake.

Which she was doing, but not in the way she needed to. Not yet. She took a sip of her white wine and let it sit on her tongue for a moment while she sorted the flavors—the base notes were of wood and smoke while the top notes were floral. Delicious. Her nose was far better than her taste buds, but she could still sort flavors fairly well by taste.

"You really are fresh off the family farm," he said.

But it wasn't an insult, not this time, and she didn't take it as such. He seemed rather…wondering, truthfully. "I suppose I am," she replied.

"With big New York dreams." His tone was a bit less friendly this time, but she didn't let it bother her. Or maybe it was the wine that didn't let it bother her.

She shrugged. "Doesn't everyone have dreams?"

His gaze slipped over her face, and she felt heat curling in her belly, her toes. Oh, how she never wanted this night to end. She wanted to drink champagne under the stars, and she wanted to dance in his arms until dawn.

His hand settled over hers, and a shiver prickled down her spine. A delicious shiver. Her entire body seemed to cant toward him, like a flower turning to the sun. His fingers skimmed along her bare arm. Fire danced in their wake, and Holly wasn't certain she could pull in her next breath.

"I have a dream," he said softly, his body so close to hers now, his beautiful mouth within reach if only she leaned a bit farther forward. His fingers slid along her cheek, into her hair, and she felt as if she were melting. She ached and wanted and didn't care what tomorrow brought so long as this man kissed her now. Tonight.

His lips hovered over hers and her eyes slid closed. Her heart was beating so hard he must surely see the pulse in her throat. But she didn't care. She was too caught up in the beauty, the wonder, the perfection of this night. It was like a fairy tale, and she was the princess who'd finally been found by the prince.

His laugh was soft and deep. It vibrated through her, made her shudder with longing.

And then his mouth claimed hers in a tender kiss that stole her breath away. It was so sweet, so perfect—

But she wanted more. She leaned closer, and he laughed again, in his throat this time, before he parted her lips and thrust his tongue into her mouth. Holly couldn't stop the moan that vibrated in her throat.

The kiss suddenly changed, turned more demanding then as his mouth took hers in a hot, possessive kiss unlike anything she'd ever experienced before. Their tongues met, tangled, dueled. She could feel the strength of that kiss in her nipples, between her legs. Her sex throbbed and her panties grew damp.

She wanted to be closer to him. Needed to be closer. She wrapped her arms around his neck, clinging to him, losing herself in this kiss, this moment.

Drago finally dragged himself up, away from her, breaking the kiss. Her mouth tingled with the memory of his. Her eyes settled on his mouth, and a thrill went through her.

"My dream," he said, his voice a sensual purr in her ear, "is that you will accompany me back to my apartment."

Holly could only stare at him as he stood and held his hand out. Everything in her wanted to be with him. She wasn't ready for this night to end, no matter that a tiny corner of her soul urged her to be cautious. She wanted more of this excitement, this exhilaration.

More of Drago.

Holly put her hand in his, and her skin sizzled at the contact. This was right, she knew it deep down. So very right.

"Yes," she said shyly. "I want that, too."

CHAPTER TWO

One year later...

"I DON'T KNOW why you don't march right into his office and demand he help you out."

Holly looked up at her best friend and roommate. Gabriella was holding little Nicholas, rocking him back and forth. He was, thankfully, asleep for a change. Poor Gabi was such a saint, considering that Nicky hadn't slept a whole night through since Holly had brought him home from the hospital.

Holly picked up a tester and sniffed it. Attar of roses. It filled her mind with a profusion of fat red blooms like the ones that her gran had grown. Bushes that now belonged to someone else, since she'd lost the property months ago. Her mouth twisted as bitterness flooded her throat with scalding acid.

She set the tester down and pushed back from the table where she mixed her fragrances. "I can't go to him, Gabi. He made it very clear that he wanted nothing more to do with me."

Holly still felt the sting of Drago di Navarra's rejection as if it was yesterday. She also—damn him—felt the utter perfection of his lovemaking as if it had happened only hours ago. Why did her body still insist on a physical response at the thought of that single night they'd shared?

At least her brain was on the right track. The only response her brain had was rage. No, that wasn't quite true. Her mental response was like a fine perfume. The top note was rage. The middle, or heart note, was self-loathing. And the base note, the one that had never yet evaporated, was shame.

How had she let herself be so damn naive and needy? How had she fallen into Drago's arms as if it were the easiest thing in the world when it was nothing like her to do so? Holly pressed her teeth together. She would never be that foolish again. She'd learned her lesson, thanks to Drago, and she would never forget it.

She'd been so easily led, so gullible and trusting. She hated thinking about it, and yet she couldn't quite stop. And maybe that was a good thing, because it meant she would never be that foolish again. The world was a cold, hard, mean place—and she was a survivor. Drago had taught her that.

He'd taught her to be suspicious and careful, to question people's motives—especially men's. He'd made her into this cold, guarded creature, and she hated him for it.

But as she looked at her son in her friend's arms, she was overcome with a sudden rush of love. Nicky was perfect. He made her world full and bright and wonderful. Every single inch of him was amazing, regardless that his father was an arrogant, evil, heartless bastard. Drago might have been the worst thing to ever happen to her, but Nicky was the best.

Irony at its most potent.

"But if he knew about Nicky," Gabi started.

"No." Holly knew her voice was hard. Thinking about Drago did that to her. But she couldn't take it out on Gabi. She tried again, sighing softly, spreading her hands wide in supplication. "I tried to tell him. His secretary said he did not want to speak to me. Ever. I wrote a letter, but I never got a reply."

Gabi looked militant. "These are the modern ages, honey bun," she said. "Put it on Facebook. Tweet the crap out of it. He'll see it and come."

Holly shuddered. As if she would expose herself that way. "He won't. Not only that, but do you want me to die of shame?" She shook her head emphatically. "No way. He had his chance."

Gabi gazed down at the cherubic face of Holly's son. "I know. But this little guy ought to have the best that money can buy."

Holly felt the truth of that statement like a barb. She couldn't help but look around their tiny apartment. Tears pricked her eyes. Since returning home to New Hope, she'd lost Gran's home, failed in her goal to become a respected perfumer and had to move sixty miles away to New Orleans so she could support herself. She'd taken a job as a cocktail waitress in a casino. It wasn't ideal, but the tips were good.

Gabi had moved last year, before Gran had died, and when Holly found out she was pregnant, Gabi had encouraged Holly to come join her.

Holly had gratefully done so.

There was no way she could stay in New Hope. Her grandmother had been a well-respected member of the community. And though Gran would have stood beside her if she'd still been alive, she wasn't. And Holly wouldn't shame her memory by causing the tongues of New Hope's citizenry to wag.

In New Hope, everyone knew everyone. And they didn't hesitate to talk about anyone so silly as to fall from grace in such a spectacular manner. Besides, no way was she subjecting Nicky to the town's censure when there was absolutely no reason for it. This was the twenty-first century, but there were those in her hometown who acted as if a single mother was a disgrace.

"I'm doing the best I can," Holly said.

Gabi's big blue eyes widened. "Oh, honey, of course you are. I'm sorry for being such an insensitive bitch." She kissed Nicky's tiny forehead. "I just forgot myself in my fury for this precious little thing. What a stupid father he has. Hopefully, when he grows up one day to be president of the United States, he won't be hampered by that side of the family tree."

Holly laughed. Leave it to Gabi to find just the thing to make her giggle when she was so angry. She went over and squeezed her friend's arm. "You're the best, Gabi. I'm not mad at you, believe me. It'll all be fine. I'm going to make a fragrance that knocks *someone's* socks off, and then I'm going to get noticed. Drago di Navarra isn't the only cosmetic king in the world, no matter what he might think."

"He messed up when he sent you home without sampling your fragrance."

The heat of shame bloomed inside her chest again. Yes, he'd sent her home without even sampling the first fragrance. After their gorgeous night together, he'd made her breakfast and served it to her in bed. She'd felt so happy, so perfectly wonderful. They'd talked and eaten and then he'd had her case delivered to her when she'd remembered to ask for it. That was when he'd noticed the scent.

"What is this, *cara*?" he'd asked, his beautiful brows drawn down in confusion as he'd studied the case in his hands.

"Those are my samples," she'd said, her heart beginning to trip in excitement.

"Samples?"

"Yes, my fragrances. I make perfume."

She'd missed the dangerous gleam in his eye as he'd set the case down and opened it. He'd drawn out a bottle of Colette and held it up, his gray eyes narrowed as he'd studied the golden fragrance.

"Explain," he'd said, his voice tight.

She'd been somewhat confused, but she had done so. Because they'd spent a beautiful night together and she knew he wasn't really an ogre. He was a passionate, sensual, good man who felt things deeply and who didn't open up easily.

Holly resisted the urge to clutch her hand over her heart, to try to contain the sharp slice of pain she still felt every time she thought of what had happened next. Of how stupid she'd been not to see it coming. She could still see his handsome face drawn up in rage, his eyes flashing hot as his jaw worked. She'd been alarmed and confused all at once.

Then he'd dropped the bottle back into the case with a clink and shoved it toward her.

"Get out," he'd said, his voice low and hard and utterly frightening.

"But, Drago—"

"Get the hell out of my home and don't come back." And then, before she could say another word, he'd stalked from the room, doors slamming behind him until she knew he was gone. A few minutes later, a uniformed maid had come in, her brow pleated in mute apology. She'd had Holly's suit—the suit she'd worn to see Drago in the first place—on a hanger, which she'd hung on a nearby hook.

It had seemed even shabbier and sadder than it had the day before.

"When you are ready, miss, Barnes will take you back to your lodgings."

Holly closed her eyes as she remembered that moment of utter shame. That moment when she'd realized he wasn't coming back, and that she'd failed spectacularly in her task to convince him of her worth as a perfumer.

Because she'd let herself get distracted. Because she'd been a mouse and a pushover and a foolish, foolish idiot.

She'd let Drago di Navarra make love to her, the first man ever to do so, and she'd gotten caught up in the fantasy of it. She'd believed that their chemistry was special, that the things she'd felt with him were unique, and that he'd felt them, too.

Fool.

But he'd kicked her out of his house as though she'd been a common prostitute.

And hadn't you?

A little voice always asked her that question. She wasn't blameless, after all. She'd spent close to twenty-four hours pretending to be something she wasn't in the single hope of convincing the high and mighty CEO of Navarra Cosmetics that she had what it took to design a signature perfume for his company.

She'd had opportunity enough to tell him why she was really there, and she'd kept silent each and every time. She'd treated it all like an adventure. The country mouse goes to the city and gets caught up in a comedy of errors. Except, she wasn't a mouse and she had a voice.

Worse, she'd complicated everything when she'd fallen for his seduction. She knew very well how it must have looked to him, a powerful man who held the key to her dream in his hand.

He'd thought her the worst kind of liar and gold digger—and the evidence had been stacked against her.

She gazed at her son and her heart felt so full with all the love swelling inside it. Yes, she should have told Drago who she was and what she wanted. But if she'd opened her mouth sooner, she wouldn't have Nicky. What a thought that was. Life might have been easier, but it certainly wouldn't have been sweeter.

Holly's eyes prickled with tears. Gran would have told

her that the past was just that and it did no good to dwell on it, because you couldn't change it without a time machine. Holly knuckled her tears away with a little laugh—but then her gaze caught on the digital display on the microwave.

"I have to get to work," she said to Gabi. "Will you be all right until Mrs. Turner comes to collect him?"

Gabi looked up from where she was still cradling Nicky. "It's a couple of hours before my shift yet. Don't worry."

Holly always worried, but she didn't say that to Gabi. She worried about providing for her baby, worried that he was only three months old and she had to work so much. She worried that she'd been unable to breast-feed him— some women couldn't, the nurse had told her after the zillionth failed attempt—and he had to drink formula, and she worried that he needed so many things and she could barely provide any of them.

Holly kissed her son's sweet soft skin before changing into her uniform of white shirt, bow tie and tight black skirt. Then she stuffed her heels into her duffel and slipped on her tennis shoes. She made it to the bus stop in record time. With twenty minutes to spare, she got to the casino, put on her heels and touched up her makeup before stashing her things and heading to the floor for her shift.

In all her wildest imaginings, she'd never pictured herself serving drinks in a casino. But here she was, arranging her tray with cocktail napkins, pen and pad, stirrers, and then gliding through the crowd of people hovering around tables and machines, asking for drink orders—and enduring a few pats to the bottom in the process.

Holly gritted her teeth, hating that part of the job but unwilling to react, because she needed the money too badly. The rent was due next week, and it was always a struggle to make up her portion along with buying diapers and formula and groceries.

Holly pushed a hand through her hair, anchoring it behind her ears, and approached the group of men hovering around one of the baccarat tables. They were rapt on the game, and most especially on a man who sat at one end of the table, a dark-haired beauty hanging over his shoulder and whispering something in his ear. His face was remarkable, beautiful and perfectly formed—and all too familiar.

For a moment, Holly was stunned into immobility. What were the chances Drago di Navarra would walk into this casino and sit at a table in her section? She'd have guessed they were something like a million to one—but here he was in all his arrogant, rotten glory.

Just her miserable luck. She glanced behind her, looking for Phyllis, hoping to ask the other waitress to take this table. Holly's belly churned and panic rose in her throat at the thought of waiting on Drago and his mistress.

But Phyllis was nowhere to be seen, and Holly had no choice. The moment she accepted that, another feeling began to boil inside her: anger.

She suddenly wanted to march over to Drago's side and slap his handsome face. She'd endured a twenty-three-hour labor, with Gabi as the only friend by her side. Other women had happy husbands in the delivery room, and masses of family in the waiting room. But not her. She'd been alone, with only Gabi holding her hand and coaching her through.

By the time Nicky had been born and someone handed him to her, she'd felt as if the little crying bundle was an alien life-form. But she'd fallen into deep love in the next moment. She had seen Drago in her son's face, and she'd felt a keen despair that he'd tossed her out the way he had. That he'd refused to take her calls. He was missing out on something amazing and perfect, and he would never know it.

Now, seeing him in this casino, sitting there so arrogant and sure with a woman hanging on him, all Holly felt was righteous anger. Her heart throbbed in her chest. Her blood beat in her brain. She knew she should turn around and walk away, find Phyllis no matter how long these people had to wait for drinks, but she couldn't seem to do it. Instead, she moved around the table until she was standing beside the man who sat at a right angle to Drago.

"Something from the bar, sir?" she asked when the play had finished. She pitched her voice louder than she normally would and looked over at Drago. The woman with him sensed a disturbance in the perfumed air around her—much too heavy a scent, Holly thought derisively, like something one would use in a brothel to cover the smells of sex and sweat—and brought her head up to meet Holly's stare.

Sweat and sex. Holly swallowed as a pinprick of hot jealousy speared into her at the thought of this woman and Drago tangling together in a bed.

Holly sniffed. No, not jealousy. As if she cared. *Honestly.*

She was irritated, that was what. Irritated by the haughty look of this woman, and the outrageous presence of the man sitting at the table, oblivious to the currents whipping in the air around him.

The woman's dark eyes raked over her. And then she did the one thing Holly had both hoped and feared she would do. She said something to Drago. He looked up, his gaze colliding with Holly's. Her heart dived into her toes at the intensity of that gray stare. A hot well of hate bubbled inside her soul. It took everything she had not to throw her tray at him and curse him for the arrogant bastard he was.

"Dry martini," the man beside her said, and Holly dragged her attention back to him.

"Yes, sir," she said, writing the drink on her pad.

When she looked up again, Drago was still looking at

her, his brows drawn together as if he were trying to place her. He didn't know her? He couldn't remember?

That was not at all the reaction she'd expected, and it pierced her to the core. She'd had his baby, and he couldn't even remember her face....

That, Holly decided, stiffening her spine, was the last straw. She turned and marched away from the table, perilously close to hyperventilating because she was so angry—and because the adrenaline rush of fear was still swirling inside her. She went over to the bar and placed her orders, telling herself to calm down and breathe.

So he didn't recognize her. So what? Had she really thought he would?

Yes.

She shook her head angrily. He was a rich, arrogant, low-down, lying son of a bitch anyway. He'd wined her and dined her and seduced her. Yes, she'd fallen for it. She wasn't blameless.

But he'd promised to take care of the birth control, and she'd trusted him to do it right. But he must have done something wrong, because she'd gotten pregnant. And he hadn't cared enough about the possibility to take her calls.

Rotten, selfish, self-serving *bastard!*

Holly grabbed her tray once the drinks were ready. She would march back over there and deliver her drinks as usual. She would *not* pour them in Drago's lap, no matter how much she wanted to.

"Thanks, Jerry," she said to the bartender. She turned to go—and nearly collided with the slickly expensive fabric of Drago di Navarra's tailored suit.

Drago's nostrils flared as he looked at the woman before him. The color in her cheeks was high as she righted her tray before spilling the contents down the front of his

Savile Row suit. Her eyes snapped fire at him and her mouth twisted in a frown.

"If you will excuse me, sir, I have drinks to deliver."

Her voice was harder than he remembered it. Her face and body were plumper, but in a good way. She'd needed to round out her curves, though he'd thought she was perfectly well formed at the time. This extra weight, however, made her into a sultry, beautiful woman rather than a naive girl.

A girl who'd tried to trick him. He hadn't forgotten that part. His jaw hardened as he remembered the way she'd so blissfully confessed her deception to him. She'd come to New York armed with perfume samples that she hoped to sell to his company, and she'd cost him valuable time and money with her pretense. It wasn't the first time a woman had tried to use him for her own ends, but it had been a pretty spectacular failure on his part. He'd had to scrap every picture from the photo shoot and start again with a new model, which had been a shame when he'd seen the photos and realized how perfect she'd been in the role.

He'd wondered in the weeks after she'd gone if he'd overreacted. But she'd scraped a raw nerve inside him, a nerve that had never healed, and throwing her out had been the right thing to do. How dare she remind him of the things he most wanted to forget?

Still, it had taken him weeks to find the right model. Even then, he hadn't actually been the one to do it. He'd been so discouraged that he'd delegated the task to his marketing director. It wasn't like him to let anything derail him for long, but every time he'd tried to find someone, he kept thinking about this woman and how she'd nearly made a fool of him.

How she'd taken him back to a dark, lonely place in his life, for the barest of moments, and made him remember what it was like to be a pawn in another's game. He shook those feelings off and studied her.

The model they'd hired to replace her was beautiful, and the fragrance was selling well, but he still wasn't satisfied. He should be, but he wasn't.

There was something about this woman. Something he hadn't quite forgotten over the past year. Even now, his body responded with a mild current of heat that he did not feel when Bridgett, whom he'd left fuming at the baccarat table, draped herself over him.

"The perfume business did not work out for you, I take it?" he asked mildly, his veins humming with predatory excitement. She was still beautiful, still the perfect woman for his ad campaign. It irritated him immensely.

And intrigued him, as well.

Her pretty blue eyes were hard beneath the dark eye makeup and black liner, but they widened when he spoke. She narrowed them again. "Not yet," she said coolly. "I'm surprised you remembered."

"I never forget a face." He let his gaze fall to her lush breasts, straining beneath the fabric of the tight white shirt the casino made her wear. "Or a body."

Her chin lifted imperiously. He would have laughed had he not sensed the loathing behind that gaze. Her plan hadn't worked and now she hated him. How droll.

"Well, isn't that fortunate for you?" she said, her Southern accent drawing out the word *you*. "If you will excuse me, sir, I have work to do."

"Still angry with me, *cara?* How odd."

She blinked. "Odd? You seduced me," she said, lowering her voice to a hiss. "And then you threw me out."

Drago lifted an eyebrow. She was a daring little thing. "You cost me a lot of money with your deception, *bella mia*. I also had to throw out a day's worth of photos and start over. Far more regrettable than tossing you out the door, I must admit."

The corners of her mouth looked pinched. But then she snorted. "I'm waiting tables in a casino and you talk to me about money? Please."

"Money is still money," he said. "And I don't like to lose it."

She was trembling, but he knew it wasn't fear that caused it. "Let me tell you something, Mr. Di Navarra," she began in a diamond-edged voice. "I made a mistake, but it cost me far more than it cost you. When you spend every last penny you have to get somewhere, because you've staked your entire future on one meeting with someone important, and then you fail in your goal and lose your home, and then have to provide for your—"

She stopped, closed her eyes and swallowed. When she opened them again, they were hot and glittering. "When you fail so spectacularly that you've lost everything and then find yourself at rock bottom, working in a casino to make ends meet, then you can be indignant, okay? Until then, spare me your wounded act."

She brushed past him, her tray balanced on one hand as she navigated the crowd to deliver her drinks. Drago watched her go, his blood sizzling. She was hot and beautiful and defiant, and she intrigued him more than he cared to admit.

In fact, she excited him in a way that Bridgett, and any of the other women he'd dated recently, did not. And, damn her, she was still perfect for the ad campaign. She wasn't quite as fresh-faced as she'd been a year ago, but she now had something more. Some quality he couldn't quite place his finger on but that he wanted nevertheless.

And he always got what he wanted, no matter the cost. He stood there with eyes narrowed, watching her deliver drinks with a false smile pasted on her face. There was something appealing about Holly Craig, something exciting.

He intended to find out what it was. And then he intended to harness it for his own purposes.

CHAPTER THREE

HOLLY'S SHIFT ENDED at one in the morning. She changed her shoes and grabbed her duffel before heading out to catch the streetcar. Once she'd ridden the streetcar as far as she could go, she would catch the bus the rest of the way home. It was a long, tiring ride, but she had no choice. It was what she could afford.

She exited the casino and started down the street. A car passed her, and then another pulled alongside. Her heart picked up, but she refused to look. The streetcar wasn't far and she didn't want to cause trouble for herself by glaring at a jerk in a sedan. It wasn't the first time some guy thought he could pick her up, and it probably wouldn't be the last.

"Would you like a ride?"

Holly's heart lurched. She stopped and turned to stare at the occupant of the gleaming limousine. He sat in the back, the window down, an arm resting casually on the sill.

"No," she said, starting to walk again. Her blood simmered. So many things she'd wanted to say to this arrogant bastard earlier, but she'd held her tongue.

Which was necessary, she realized. It would do no good to antagonize Drago di Navarra. Not only that, but there was also a little prickle of dread growing in her belly at the thought of him learning about Nicky. No doubt he would think she'd done that on purpose, too.

Which was ridiculous, considering he'd been the one to assure her that birth control was taken care of.

"It's late and you must be tired," he said, his voice so smooth and cultured. Oh, how she hated those dulcet Italian tones!

"I am tired," she told him without looking at him. The limo kept pace with her as she walked, and it irritated her to think of him sitting there so comfortably while she trod on aching feet across the pavement. "But I'm tired every night and I manage. So thanks anyway."

Drago laughed softly. "So spirited, Holly. Nothing at all like the girl who came to New York with starry-eyed dreams of success."

A bubble of helpless anger popped low in her belly. She stopped and spun around, marching over to the car. It was completely unlike her, but she couldn't seem to stop herself. The urge to confront him was unbearable. The limo halted.

"I might have been naive then, but I'm not now. I know the world is a cruel place and that some people who have absolutely everything they could ever want are even crueler than that." She tossed a stray lock of hair over her shoulder with trembling fingers. "So if I'm *spirited*, as you say, I had to learn to be that way. It's a dog-eat-dog world, and I don't want to be eaten."

Spirited? She hardly thought of herself that way at all. No, more like she was a survivor because she had to be. Because someone else depended on her. Someone tiny and helpless.

Drago opened the car door and stepped out, and Holly took a step back. He was so tall, so broad, so perfect.

No, not perfect. A jerk!

"Get in the car, Holly," he said, his voice deep and commanding. "Don't be so stubborn."

Holly folded her arms beneath her breasts and cocked a

hip. "I don't have to do what you order me to do, Drago," she said, using his name on purpose. Reminding him they'd once been intimate and that she wasn't an employee—or, heaven forbid, a girlfriend—to be ordered around. It felt bold and wicked and brave, and that was precisely what she needed to be in order to face him right now. "Besides, won't your lady friend be angry if you drag me along for the ride?"

His nostrils flared in irritation. One thing she remembered about Drago di Navarra was that he was not accustomed to anything less than blind obedience. It gave her a sense of supreme satisfaction to thwart that expectation.

"Bridgett is no longer an issue," he said haughtily, and Holly laughed. He looked surprised.

"Poor Bridgett, tossed out on her gorgeous derriere without a clue as to what she did wrong."

Drago left the door open and came over to her. He was so tall she had to tilt her head back to look up at him. Her first instinct was to flee, but she refused to give in to it. Not happening. She'd been through too much to run away at the first sign of trouble. She told herself that she was far stronger than she'd been a year ago. She had to be.

She *was*.

"Get in the car, Holly, or I'll pick you up and toss you in it," he growled. It surprised her to realize that she could smell his anger. It was sharp and hot, with the distinct smell of a lit match.

"I'd like to see you try," she threw at him, heedless of the sizzle in his glare. "This is America, buddy, and you can't just kidnap people off the street."

Holly didn't quite know what happened next, but suddenly she was in the air, slung over his shoulder before she could do a thing to stop him.

"Put me down!" she yelled, beating her fists against his back as he carried her over to the car. The next instant, she was tilting downward again, and she clung to him as if he was going to drop her. But he tossed her into the car instead, tossed her bag in after her, and then he was inside and the door slammed shut.

Holly flung herself at the opposite door, but it was locked tight. The limo began to speed down Canal Street. Holly turned and slammed her back against the seat, glaring at the arrogant Italian billionaire sitting at the opposite end. He looked smug. And he didn't have a hair out of place, while she had to scrape a tangle of hair from her face and shove it back over her ears.

"How dare you?" she seethed. Her heart pounded and adrenaline shoved itself into her limbs, her nerves, until she felt as if she were wound so tight she would split at the seams. If his anger was a lit match, hers was a raging fire. "If anyone saw that, you're in big trouble."

"I doubt it," he said. He leaned forward then, gray eyes glittering in the darkened car. "Now, tell me where you live, Holly Craig, and my driver will take you home. Much easier, *no*?"

Holly glared.

"Come, Holly. It's late and you look tired."

She wanted to refuse—but then she rattled off her address. What choice did she have? It *was* late, she *was* tired, and she needed to get Nicky from Mrs. Turner. If she had to let this man take her there, so be it. At least she would arrive far earlier than if she took the bus. And that would make Mrs. Turner happy, no doubt.

"Do you have a guilty conscience?" she asked when he'd given the driver the address.

He laughed. "Hardly."

That stung, but she told herself she should hardly be surprised. He'd thrown her out without a shred of remorse, and then refused all attempts to contact him. Heartless man.

"Then why the sudden chivalrous offer of a ride home?"

His gaze slid over her, and her skin prickled with telltale heat. She gritted her teeth, determined not to feel even a sliver of attraction for this man. Before she'd met Drago di Navarra, she'd thought she was a sensible woman in control of her own emotions. He'd rather exploded that notion in her face.

And continued to explode it as her body reacted to his presence without regard to her feelings for him. Feelings of loathing, she reminded herself. Feelings of sheer dislike.

Her body didn't care.

"Because I need you, *cara mia*."

She swallowed the sudden lump in her throat. He'd said something similar to her that night in his apartment. And she, like an idiot, had believed him. Worse, she'd wanted it to be true. Well, she wasn't that naive anymore. Italian billionaires did not fall in love with simple, unsophisticated virgins in the space of an evening.

They didn't fall in love at all.

"Sorry, but the answer is no."

His long elegant fingers were steepled together in his lap. "You have not yet heard the proposition."

"I'm still sure the answer is no," she said. "I've been propositioned by you before, and I know how that works out for me."

He shook his head as if he were disappointed in her. "I liked you better in New York."

Her skin stung with heat. "Of course you did. I was a mouse who did whatever you told me to do. I've learned better now."

And she was determined to prove it.

"You like being a cocktail waitress, *bella*? You like men touching you, rubbing up against you, thinking you're for sale along with the drinks and the chips?"

The heat in her cheeks spread, suffusing her with an

angry glow. "No, I don't. But it's just about all I'm qualified for."

"And if I were to offer you something else? A better way to earn your money?"

Her stomach was beginning to churn. "I won't be your mistress."

He blinked at her. And then he laughed again, and she felt the hot, sticky slide of embarrassment in her veins. Oh, for pity's sake. After the way the woman he'd been with tonight looked, did she truly think he was interested in her?

But he had been once. She hadn't dreamed it. Nicky was proof she had not.

"Charming, Holly. But I don't need to pay a woman to be my mistress. If I were to choose you for that…position…I am certain you would not refuse."

Holly could only gape at his utter self-confidence. "It's a wonder you bother with casinos when you have such bad instincts. I'm surprised you haven't lost everything when you reason like that in the face of such overwhelming evidence to the contrary."

"*Dio,*" he said, "but you are a stubborn woman. How did we end up in bed together again?" He didn't wait for her reply. He nodded sagely as if answering his own question. "Ah, yes, that's right. You were deceiving me."

Shame suffused her at that mention of their night together. But she didn't bother to deny it. He wouldn't believe it anyway. "Clearly, you like your women to shut up and do as they're told."

"Which you seem to be incapable of doing," he growled.

"Fine," she snapped. "Tell me what you want so I can say no."

His stare was unnerving. But not because it made her uncomfortable. More likely because she wanted to drown in it. "I want you to model for the Sky campaign."

Holly's mouth went dry. Sky was the signature fra-

grance from NC, the one she'd modeled for in New York
when she hadn't been able to tell Drago why she was really there. "That's not funny," she said tightly.

His expression was dead serious. "I'm not joking, Holly.
I want you for Sky."

"I did that already," she said. "It didn't work out, as I
recall."

He shrugged. "A mistake. One we can rectify now."

The trembling in her belly wasn't going away. It was
spreading through her limbs, making her teeth chatter. She
clamped her jaw tight and tried not to let it show. Thankfully, the car was dark and the lights from the city didn't
penetrate the tinted windows quite as well as they otherwise would have.

"I don't think it's possible," she said. And it wasn't.
How would she go to New York with a three-month-old
baby in tow? She didn't think that was what Drago had
in mind at all.

"Of course it is. I will pay you far more than you earn
in that casino. You will do the shoot and any appearances
that are needed, and you will be handsomely rewarded.
It's a win for you, Holly."

She thought of her baby in his secondhand crib, of the
tiny, dingy apartment she shared with Gabi. The air con-
ditioner was one window unit that rattled and coughed so
badly she was never certain it would keep working. The
carpet was faded and torn, and the appliances were always
one usage away from needing repairs.

It was a dump, a dive, and she would do just about anything to get out of there and take her baby to a better life.

But what if he didn't mean it? What if he was toying
with her? What if this was simply another way to punish
her for not telling him the truth in New York?

She wouldn't put it past him. A man who threw her out
and then refused all contact? Who didn't know he had

a son, because he was so damn arrogant as to think she would want to contact him for any other reason than to tell him something important?

He was capable of it. More than capable.

"I want a contract," she said. "I want everything spelled out, legal and binding, and if it's legit, then I'll do it."

Because what choice did she have? She wasn't stupid, and she wasn't going to turn this opportunity down when it could mean everything to her child. Once she had a contract, signed and ironclad, she would feel much more in control.

"Fine."

Holly blinked. She hadn't expected him to agree to that.

"I hope you're certain about this," she said, unable to help herself when her teeth were still chattering and her body still trembling. What if this was a mistake? What if she were opening up Pandora's box with this act? How could she *not* be opening Pandora's box, when she had a three-month-old baby, and this man didn't know he was a father? "You know I'm not a model. I have no idea what I'm doing."

"Which is precisely why you're correct for the campaign. Sky is for the real woman who wants to recapture a certain something about her life. Her youth, her innocence, her sex appeal."

Irritation slid into her veins. "I've smelled Sky. It's not bad, but it's not all that, either."

The match-scent of anger rolled from him again. Why, oh, why did she feel the need to antagonize him? *Just take the money and shut up*, she told herself. The silence between them was palpable. And then he spoke. "Ah, yes, because you are an expert perfumer, correct?"

Sarcasm laced his voice. It made her madder than she already was, regardless that she knew she shouldn't push him.

"You have no idea. As I recall, you threw me out before I could show you."

He sat back in the limo then, his long limbs relaxing as if he were about to take a nap. She knew better, though. He was more like a panther, stretching out and pretending to relax when what he really planned was to bring down a gazelle.

"It takes years to learn how to blend perfumes. It also takes very intense training, and a certain sensitivity to smell. While you may have enjoyed mixing up essences you've ordered off the internet for all your friends, and while many of them may have told you how fabulous you are, that's hardly the right sort of training to create perfume for a multinational conglomerate, now, is it?"

Rage burned low in her belly, along with a healthy dose of uncertainty. It wasn't that she wasn't good, but she often felt the inadequacy of her origins in the business. She had no curriculum vitae, no discernable job experience. How could she communicate to anyone that she was worthy of a chance without backing it up with fragrance samples?

She glanced out the window, but they weren't quite to her neighborhood yet. So she turned back to him and tried very hard not to tell him to go to hell. He was so arrogant, so certain of himself.

And she suddenly burned to let him know it.

"It's gratifying that you know so much about me already," she said, a razor edge to her voice. "But perhaps you didn't know that my grandmother was born in Grasse and trained there for years before she met her husband and moved to Louisiana. She gave up her dreams of working for a big house, but she never gave up the art. And she taught it to me."

It wasn't the kind of formal instruction he would expect, but Gran had been extremely good at what she did. And Holly was, too.

She heard him pull in a breath. "That may be, but it still does not make you an expert, *bella mia.*"

The accusation smarted. "Again, until you've tried my scents, you can't really know that, can you?" She crossed her arms and tilted up her chin. Hell, why not go for it? What did she have to lose? "In fact, I want that in the contract. You will allow me to present my work to you if I model for your campaign."

He laughed softly. The sound scraped along her nerve endings. But not quite in a bad way. No, it was more like heated fingers stroking her sensitive skin. She wanted more.

"You realize that I will say yes to this, don't you? But why not? It costs me nothing. I can still say no to your fragrances, even if I agree to let you show them to me."

"I'm aware of that."

She believed him to be too good a businessman to turn her fragrances away out of spite. He hadn't built Navarra Cosmetics into what it was today by being shortsighted. She was counting on that.

And yet there was much more at risk here, wasn't there? They were getting closer and closer to her home, and she had a baby that was one half of his DNA.

But why should that matter?

He was the sperm donor. *She* was the one who'd sacrificed everything to take care of her child. She was the one who'd gone through her entire pregnancy alone and with only a friend for support. She was the one who'd brought him into the world, and the one who sat up with him at night, who worried about him and who loved him completely.

This man hadn't cared enough about the possibility of a child to allow her even to contact him. He'd thrown her out and self-importantly gone about his life as if she'd never existed.

A life that had included many trysts with models and actresses. Oh, yes, she'd known all about that even when she hadn't wanted to. His beautiful, deceptive face had stared out at her from the pages of the tabloids in the checkout line. While she'd been buying the few necessities she could afford to keep herself alive and healthy, he'd been wining and dining supermodels in Cannes and Milan and Venice.

She'd despised him for so long that to be with him now, in this car, was rather surreal. She had a baby with him, but she didn't think he'd like that at all. And she wasn't going to tell him. He'd done nothing to deserve to know.

Nothing except father Nicky.

She shoved that thought down deep and slapped a lid on it. Yes, she absolutely believed that a man ought to know he had a child. But she couldn't quite get there with Drago di Navarra. He wasn't just any man.

Worse, he'd probably decide she was trying to deceive him again, and then her chances of earning any money to take care of her baby would be nullified before she ever stepped in front of a camera. He'd throw her and Nicky to the wolves without a second thought, and then he'd step into his fancy limo and be ferried away to the next amazingly expensive location on his To See list.

No, she couldn't tell him. She couldn't take the chance when there was finally a light at the end of the tunnel.

The car pulled to a stop in front of her shabby apartment building. Drago looked out the window—at the yellow lights staining everything in a sickly glow, the fresh graffiti sprayed across the wall of a building opposite, the overflowing garbage bins waiting for tomorrow's pickup, the skinny dog pulling trash from one of them—and stiffened.

"You cannot stay here," he said, his voice low and filled with horror.

Holly sucked in a humiliated breath. It looked bad, yes, but the residents here were good, honest people. There were drugs in the neighborhood, but not in this building. Mr. Boudreaux ran it with an iron fist. It was the safest thing she could afford. Shame crawled down her spine at the look on Drago's face.

"I *am* staying here," she said quietly. "And I thank you for the ride home."

His gaze swung toward her. "It's not safe here, *bella mia.*"

Holly gritted her teeth. "I've been living here for the past seven months," she said. "It's where I live. It's what I can afford. And you have no idea about safe. You're only assuming it's not because it's not a fancy New York neighborhood like you're used to."

He studied her for a long moment. And then he pressed an intercom button and spoke to the driver in Italian. After that, he swung the door open and stepped out.

"Come then. I will walk you to your apartment."

"You don't have to do that," she protested, joining him on the pavement with her duffel in tow. "The door is right here."

The building was two stories tall, with three entrances along its front. Each stairwell had two apartments on each floor. Hers was on the second floor, center stairwell. And the driver had parked the limo right in front of it. A dog barked—not the one in the garbage, but a different one—and a curtain slid back. She could see Mrs. Landry's face peering outside. When her gaze landed on the limousine, the light switched out and Holly knew the old woman had turned it off so she could see better.

She was a nosy lady, but a sweet one.

"I insist," Drago said, and Holly's heart skipped a beat. She had to take her things to her apartment, and then she had to go to Mrs. Turner's across the hall and get Nicky.

"Fine," she said, realizing he wasn't going away otherwise. If she let him walk her to the door, he'd be satisfied, even if he walked her up the steps to her apartment. And it wasn't as if her baby was home.

She turned and led the way to the door. She reached to yank it open, but he was there first, pulling it wide and motioning for her to go inside.

"Better be careful you don't get your fancy suit dirty coming inside here," she said.

"I know a good cleaner," he replied, and she started up the stairs—quietly, so as not to alert Mrs. Turner, who might just come to the door with her baby if she heard Holly arrive.

He followed her in silence until she reached the landing and turned around to face him. He was two steps behind her, and it put him on eye level with her. The light from the stairwell was sickly, but she didn't think there was a light on this earth that wouldn't love Drago di Navarra. It caressed his cheekbones, the aristocratic blade of his nose, shone off the dark curls of his hair. His mouth was flat and sensual, his lips full, and she remembered with a jolt what it had felt like to press her lips to his.

Dammit.

"This is it," she whispered. "You can go now."

He didn't move. "Open the door, Holly. I want to make certain you get inside."

He didn't whisper, and she shot a worried glance at Mrs. Turner's door. She could hear the television, and she knew her neighbor was awake.

"Shh," she told him. "People are sleeping. These walls are thin, which I am sure you aren't accustomed to, but—"

He moved then, startling her into silence as he came up to the landing and took her key from her limp hand. "You'd be surprised what I have been accustomed to, *cara*," he said shortly. "Now, tell me which door before I choose one."

Her skin burned. She pointed to her door and stood

silently by while he unlocked it and stepped inside. Humiliation was a sharp dagger in her gut then. A year ago, he'd dressed her in beautiful clothes, made her the center of attention, taken her to a restaurant she could never in a million years afford and then taken her back to his amazing Park Avenue apartment with the expansive view of Central Park. None of those things was even remotely like what he would see inside her apartment and she burned with mortification at what he must be thinking.

He turned back to her, his silvery eyes giving nothing away. "It appears to be safe," he told her, standing back so she could enter her own home. A home that, she knew, would have fit into the foyer of his New York apartment.

She slid the door quietly closed behind her, not because she wanted to shut him in, but because she wanted to keep her presence from Mrs. Turner until he was gone.

Fury slid into her bones, permeating her, making her shake with its force. She spun on him and jerked her keys from his hand. "How dare you?" she sputtered. "How dare you assume that because I live in a place that doesn't meet with your approval, you have a right to think I need your help to enter my own home?"

"Just because you've entered without incident in the past doesn't mean there won't come a night when someone has broken in to wait for you," he grated. "You're on the second floor, *cara*. You're a beautiful woman, living alone, and—" here he pointed "—these windows aren't precisely security windows, are they? So forgive me if I wanted to make sure you were safe. I could no more allow you to come in here alone than I could jump out that window and fly. It's not what a man does."

"First of all, I don't see why you care. And second, I don't live alone," she grated in return, her heart thrumming at everything he'd just said.

He blinked. "You have a boyfriend?"

"A best friend, if you must know. And she's at work right now."

He glanced around the room again. Gabi had left a lamp burning, as she always did, but it was a dim one in order to save electricity. Drago flicked a switch on the wall, and the overhead light popped on, revealing the apartment in all its shabby glory.

It was clean, but worn. And there was no way to hide that. His gaze slid over the room—and landed squarely on the package of diapers and jars of baby food sitting on the dinette. Holly closed her eyes and cursed herself for not putting everything away this afternoon. She'd been too caught up with her fragrances in the little free time she'd had after returning from the store.

Drago's brows drew down as he turned his head toward her. "You have a baby in this apartment?"

Before she could answer him, tell him she was collecting for charity or something, there was a knock on the door.

"Holly?" Mrs. Turner called. "Are you home, sweetie?"

CHAPTER FOUR

DRAGO WATCHED AS the color drained from Holly Craig's face. She pushed her hair behind her ear and turned away from him, toward the door.

"Coming, Mrs. Turner," she said sweetly, and he felt a flicker of annoyance. She'd been nothing but cross with him since the moment he'd first spoken to her in the casino. He understood why she would be angry with him, since he'd ruined her plans last year, but she should be perfectly amenable now that he was offering her the job of modeling for Sky. If she was ambitious, and she must be to undergo the deception she had, why wasn't she softening toward him?

His gaze landed on a table tucked into one corner of the room. It was lined with testers and other paraphernalia she must use to make her fragrance. Clearly, she was serious about it. And her grandmother was from Grasse, the perfume capital of the world. That didn't mean the woman had had any talent, or that she'd been a *nez*. Those were highly prized. If she'd been a nose, she would have gone to work in the industry, husband or no.

But Holly was certainly convinced she had what it took to succeed in his business. He glanced at the shabby furnishings and wasn't persuaded. If she had talent, why was she here? Why hadn't she kept trying even after he'd turned her down? There were other companies, other opportunities. They weren't the best, but they were a leg up.

Which she desperately seemed to need, he admitted. He refused to feel any remorse for that. She might have spent all her money coming to New York, but he was not responsible for her choices.

And yet, this place depressed him. Made him feel jumpy and angry and insignificant in ways he'd thought he'd forgotten long ago. He hadn't always lived the way he did now—with everything money could buy at his fingertips—and this dingy apartment was far too familiar. He thought of his mother and her insane quest for something he'd never understood—something she'd never understood, either, he'd finally come to realize years after the fact.

Donatella Benedetti had been looking for enlightenment, the best he could figure. And she'd been willing to drag her only son from foreign location to foreign location, some of them without electricity or running water or any means of communicating with the world at large. He'd held a hat while she'd busked on the streets, playing a violin with adequate-enough skill to gain a few coins for a meal. He'd curled up in a canoe while they'd floated down an Asian river, moving toward a village of mud huts and deprivation. He'd learned to beg for money by looking pitiful and small and hungry. He'd known how to count coins before he'd ever learned to read.

Holly took a deep breath and opened the door to greet an older woman standing on the other side. The woman held a baby carrier, presumably containing a baby, if the way Holly bent down and looked at it was any indication.

The beginnings of a headache started to throb in Drago's temple. Babies were definitely not his thing. They were tiny and mysterious and needy, and he hadn't a clue what to do with them.

"I thought I heard you come up," the woman was saying. "He was a good baby tonight. Such a sweetie."

"Thank you, Mrs. Turner. I really appreciate you helping out like this."

The other woman waved a hand. "Pish. You know I'm a night owl. It's no problem to keep him while you work." She looked up then, her gaze landing on him. Drago inclined his head while her eyes drifted over him. "Oh, my, I didn't know you had company," she said.

Holly turned briefly and then waved a hand as if to dismiss him. "Just an old acquaintance I ran into tonight. He's leaving now."

He was not leaving, but he didn't bother to tell her that. Or, he was leaving, but not just yet. Not until he figured out what was happening here.

There was a baby, in a carrier, and Holly was taking it from the woman. Was it her baby? Or her roommate's? And did it matter? So long as she modeled for Sky, did he care?

"Go ahead and take care of the baby," he said evenly. "I can go in a moment, once everything is settled."

The woman she'd called Mrs. Turner nodded approvingly. "Excellent idea. Get the little pumpkin settled first."

Mrs. Turner handed over a diaper bag, as well as the carrier, and Drago stepped forward to take the bag from Holly. She didn't protest, but she didn't look at him, either. A few more seconds passed as Holly and Mrs. Turner said their goodbyes, and then the door closed and they were alone.

Or, strike that, there were three of them where there'd been four. Drago gazed at the baby carrier as the child inside cooed and stretched.

"He's hungry," Holly said. "I have to feed him."

"Don't let me stop you."

She gazed at him with barely disguised hatred. "I'd

prefer you go," she said tightly. "It's late, and we need to get to bed."

"Whose baby is this?" he asked curiously. He thought of her in New York, sweet and innocent and so responsive to his caresses, and hated the idea she could have been with another man. He'd been her first. Yet another thing about her that had fooled him into thinking she hadn't had ulterior motives.

Drago tried very hard not to remember her expression of wonder when he'd entered her fully for the first time. She'd clung to him so sweetly, her body opening to him like a flower, and he'd felt an overwhelming sense of honor and protectiveness toward her. Something she'd been counting on, no doubt.

Dio, she had fooled him but good. She'd gotten past all his defenses and made him care, however briefly. Anger spun up inside him. But there were other feelings, too, desire being chief among them. It rather surprised him how sharp that feeling was, as if he'd not had sex in months rather than hours. Quite simply, he wanted to spear his hands into her hair and tilt her mouth up for his pleasure.

And then he wanted to strip her naked and explore every inch of her skin the way he once had, and let the consequences be damned.

Her expression was hard as she looked at him, and he wondered if she knew what he was thinking. Then she walked over to the couch—a distance of about four steps—and set the baby carrier on the floor. She grabbed the diaper bag from him and began to rummage in it. Soon, she had a bottle in her hands and she took the baby out of the carrier and began to feed it.

Drago watched the entire episode, a skein of discomfort uncoiling inside him as she deliberately did not answer his question.

It wasn't a hard question, but she looked down at the

baby and made faces, talking in a high voice and ignoring him completely. Her long reddish-blond hair draped over one shoulder, but she didn't push it back. He let his gaze wander her features, so pretty in a simple way, and yet earthy somehow, too.

She had not been earthy before. Now she bent over the child, holding the bottle, her full breasts threatening to burst from the white shirt, her legs long and lean beneath the tight skirt of the casino uniform. The only incongruous items of clothing were the tennis shoes she'd changed into.

Drago suddenly felt out of his element. Holly Craig nursed a child and turned every bit of love and affection she had on it, when all she could spare for him was contempt. Watching her with the baby, he had a visceral reaction that left a hole in the center of his chest. Had his mother ever focused every ounce of attention she had on him? Had she ever looked at him with such love? Or had she only ever looked at him as a burden and a means to an end?

"Holly," he said, his voice tight, and she looked up at him, her gaze defiant and hard. If he'd been a lesser man, he would have stumbled backward under that knife-edged gaze of hers. He was not a lesser man. "Whose child is that?"

He asked the question, but he was pretty certain he knew the answer by now.

"Not that it's any of your business," she told him airily, "but Nicky is mine. If this changes your plan to have me model for Sky, then I'd appreciate it if you'd get out and leave us alone."

Holly's heart hammered double-time in her chest. She hadn't wanted him to know about Nicky at all, not yet, not until the contract he'd agreed to provide was signed and she knew she'd get her money for doing the Sky campaign at the very least.

But of course her luck had run out months ago. First, she'd gone to New York, spent every dime she had and come home empty-handed. Then she'd lost the house and property—and found out she was pregnant. God, she could still remember her utter shock when her period hadn't started and she'd finally worked up the courage to buy a pregnancy test.

And she'd driven two towns over to do so, not wanting *anyone* in New Hope to wonder why she needed a pregnancy test.

She looked down at the sweet, soft baby in her arms now and knew for a fact he was not a mistake. But he'd definitely been a shock on top of everything else she'd had to deal with just then.

And now, of course, when all she wanted was the absolute best for him, when she needed to protect him and provide for him and keep him secret until she had this job sewn up, Mrs. Turner had heard her come home and brought him to her. What if Drago figured it out? What would happen then? She'd lose the opportunity to provide a better life for her baby.

Drago was looking at her with a mixture of disdain and what she thought might be utter horror. Resignation settled over her. She'd already lost the opportunity then.

But you can still tell him the truth.

Would he ignore his child's needs if he knew? Could she take that chance?

"How old is the child?" he asked, brows drawn low, and her heart did that funny squeeze thing it did when she was scared.

"A couple of months," she said vaguely, ignoring the voice. She couldn't tell him. How could she take the chance after everything that had happened? Not only that, but why did he deserve to know when he'd thrown her out and left her to fend for herself?

Guilt and fear swirled into a hot mess inside her belly. She'd always done the right thing. But what was the right thing now?

"You wasted no time, I see," he said coolly.

"I'm sorry?"

He looked hard and cool, remote. "Finding another lover," he spat at her.

A hard knot of something tightened right beneath her breastbone. Of course he thought she'd gone home and gotten pregnant by someone else. Of course he did. Holly closed her eyes and willed herself to be calm.

It didn't work.

My God, the man was arrogant beyond belief! Resentment flared to life in her gut, a hot bright fire that seared into her. "Why should I have waited? Thanks for showing me what I'd been missing, by the way. It was ever so easy to go home and climb back on the horse."

She gazed down at Nicky, who was sucking the bottle for all he was worth, and willed the irrational tears gathering behind her eyelids to melt away. Drago di Navarra not only thought she'd intended to use her body to get what she wanted out of him, but he also thought she'd been so promiscuous as to run straight home and get pregnant by another man. As if she could have borne another man's touch after she'd had his.

"Perhaps you should have been more careful," he said, and a fresh wave of hatred pounded into her. Her head snapped up. She didn't care what he saw in her gaze now.

"How dare you?" she said, her voice low and tight. "You know nothing about me. *Nothing!*" She sucked in a shaky breath. "Nicky is a gift, however he got here. I wouldn't trade him for a million Sky contracts, so you can take your disdain and your contempt and get the hell out of my home."

She was shaking, she realized, and Nicky felt it. He started to kick his little arms and legs, and his face scrunched up. The bottle popped out of his mouth, but before she could get it back in, he turned his head and started to wail.

"Shush, sweetie, Mommy's here," she crooned, her eyes stinging with tears and gritty from lack of sleep. She just wanted to put her head down and not get up again for a good long time.

But that wasn't possible. It wasn't ever possible these days.

"Forgive me. I shouldn't have said that."

Holly cuddled Nicky, rocking him softly, and looked up at Drago. Shock coursed through her system at those quiet words, uttered with sincerity. It was a glimpse of the man she'd found so compelling last year, the one who'd made her feel safe and who'd made her laugh and sigh and then shatter in his arms.

She'd liked that man, right up until the moment he'd proven he didn't really have a heart after all. And while she told herself not to be fooled now, she was moved by the apology. Or maybe she was just too exhausted to keep up the anger.

Nicky continued to wail, and Holly stood and bounced him up and down in her arms. "Hush, baby. It's okay."

"You need help," Drago said.

She didn't look at him. "I have help. You saw Mrs. Turner. Gabi helps, too. It's my turn now."

"You're tired, Holly. You should get some sleep."

"I can't sleep until he does." She paced the floor, giving Drago as wide a berth as possible in the small room. "You should probably go. Your driver will be wondering if I bashed you over the head and took your wallet."

"I doubt it," he said. He eyed the room again and she could feel the strength of his contempt for their surroundings.

"Drago." He looked at her, his nostrils flaring. He was acting as if he'd been caught with his hand in the cookie jar. "You should go. We'll be fine. We've been fine for months. Nicky will fall asleep soon, and then I'm going to crash, too. I have another shift tomorrow at noon."

"I'm afraid I can't do that," he said, and her stomach flipped. He took a step closer to her and she bounced Nicky a little more frantically. It seemed he didn't mind the movement at all. His little eyes were starting to close.

"Of course you can," she said. "You can't stay here, for God's sake. Nor would you want to, I'm sure. I'm afraid we don't have silk sheets, milord, or room service—"

"Shut up, Holly, and listen to me," he commanded.

And, as much as she wanted to tell him to go to hell, she did as he told her. Because she was tired. And scared he would walk out and take her last opportunity with him.

"I'm listening," she said when he didn't immediately continue.

"I'm returning to New York in the morning. You're coming with me."

Reflexively, she held Nicky a little tighter. "I'm not leaving my baby. Nor am I going anywhere without a contract," she said tightly. Because she didn't trust him. Because, as much as she wanted it to be true, she was too accustomed to bad luck to believe it was finally turning around for her.

Drago di Navarra wasn't suddenly being nice and accommodating for no reason. Did he suspect? Or was he just planning to drop her from an even greater height than he had the last time?

"No, you aren't leaving him," Drago said. "And you aren't returning to that casino, either. Pack what you need for the night. I'll send someone by for the rest of your things tomorrow."

Holly could only gape at him, her skin flushing hot with hope and fear and shame all rolled into one. *Don't trust him, don't trust him....*

And yet she wanted to. Needed to. He was the only way out of this hellhole.

Except, she had obligations.

"I can't just leave," she said. "This is my home. Gabi isn't even here. I can't quit the casino without notice—"

"You can," he said firmly. "You will."

Pressure was building behind her forehead. What should she do? What would Gran have said? Thoughts of Gran threatened to bring a fresh flood of tears, so she bit down on her lip and pushed them deep. *Think, Holly.*

"You're asking me to turn my life upside down for nothing more than a promise," she said. "How do I know you aren't planning some elaborate scheme to put me in my place once more?"

He blinked. And then he laughed, while she felt her skin turn even redder. "Honestly, *cara*, do you think I've spent a year plotting how to pay you back for deceiving me in New York? Until tonight, I had not given you another thought."

Well, all righty, then.

His words stung in ways she hadn't imagined possible. There wasn't a day since he'd thrown her out that she hadn't thought about him in some capacity or other—and here he was telling her so offhandedly that he hadn't thought of her at all.

"How flattering," she murmured, keeping her eyes on her baby so as not to reveal her hurt.

"It's not personal," he told her, all gorgeous Italian play-boy. "I am a busy man. But when I saw you again, I remembered those photos and how right you were in them. All I want is your face on my campaign."

Nicky was finally asleep now. Holly turned and took him into her bedroom, where she placed him in his crib near her bed. When she straightened, Drago was standing in the door.

"I'll go," she told him quietly, making her decision. "But not tonight." She turned to look back at her baby before gazing at Drago again. "He can't be moved right now. It'll wake him up. And I'm too tired to pack a thing."

She joined Drago in the entry to her room. He was gazing down at her in frustration, his brows drawn down over his beautiful gray eyes.

"You're a very stubborn woman, Holly Craig," he said softly, his eyes dipping to her mouth before coming back up again. Her lips tingled. She told herself it was because she'd been biting them.

"I will always do what's best for my baby," she said. "He comes first. I'm sorry if you find that inconvenient."

She could feel the heat of Drago's body enveloping her, smell the cool scent of his cologne—a home run for Navarra Cosmetics, at least where he was concerned. Scents smelled different on different people, but this one seemed tailored to him. It was light, so light she'd not really noticed it before now, but it was also intoxicating.

There was sandalwood, which was to be expected in male cologne. But there were also pears, which was surprising, as well as moss. It was fresh and clean and she liked it. And she would forever associate the smell of NC's signature male cologne with its ruthless CEO.

Drago's mouth flattened for a moment, as if he were annoyed. But then he shook his head slightly.

"An admirable trait in a mother, I imagine," he said, and there was a piercing pain in her heart that she did not understand. Did he sound wistful just then? Lonely? Lost?

"I will send a car for you in the morning, *cara*. Say your goodbyes and pack your things. You won't need to return to this dwelling ever again."

Her heart hammered. "I can't leave Gabi in the lurch. She will need enough money to cover a couple of months' rent at least."

He didn't even blink. "I will take care of it."

And then he was gone, his footsteps echoing in the stairwell as he left her life once more.

CHAPTER FIVE

DRAGO'S APARTMENT IN New York was somehow even grander than she remembered it. Holly lay back on a bed that was almost as big as her entire room had been in New Orleans and stared up at a ceiling that had actual frescoes painted on it. Frescoes, as if this were a grand church instead of a personal dwelling.

Stunning. And completely surreal.

It was late afternoon and she needed to get out of bed, but she didn't want to. Early this morning—far earlier than she would have liked—Nicky had been awake and ready for his bottle. While she'd fed her baby, she'd done a pretty good job of convincing herself that Drago wasn't coming back. That she'd dreamed the whole thing.

Gabi had stumbled home at six, and Holly had told her the whole story—including the part where she was supposed to leave New Orleans and never have to worry about living in squalor again.

Gabi's face had lit up like the Fourth of July. "Oh, my God, Holly, that's amazing! You have to go! You *are* going, right?"

Holly had frowned. "I'm not sure." Then she'd raked a hand through her tangle of hair. "I mean, last night I was pretty sure. But how can I leave you? And how can I possibly deal with that man again? He's not nice, Gabi. He's selfish and arrogant and only concerned with his bottom line and—"

"And handsome as sin," Gabi had interrupted. "As well as richer than God. Not to mention he's the father of your baby."

Holly had frowned. "That's what worries me the most."

Gabi had sat down and taken her hand, squeezing it. Her blue eyes had been so serious. "This is a once-in-a-lifetime opportunity, Holly. You have to go. There's a reason this is happening now, and you have to go see what it is."

In the end, Holly had gone. Drago had arrived at eight, and by then Holly had packed everything she needed into three suitcases and a diaper bag. It was everything she owned. Drago had looked over her belongings coldly, and then his driver had carried them all down to the limo. Holly had hugged Gabi goodbye, crying and promising to call. She'd been terrified to leave her friend alone, but Drago had handed Gabi a fat envelope and told her to use it wisely.

Holly had bitten her lip to keep from saying something she might regret. It was up to Gabi to accept or decline the money, and in the end she'd accepted. She'd had no choice, really. Without Holly to help with expenses, she would have had to hustle to find another roommate or take on extra hours at work. The money was the better choice.

Within an hour, they'd been on a plane to New York. Within two hours, they'd landed. And, an hour later, she'd found herself in this room. She didn't know what she'd expected, but staying at Drago's had not been it. When she'd turned to him, he'd known what she was going to say, because he'd preempted her.

"There's no sense putting you in a hotel with a baby when this place is so big."

Nicky was in an adjoining room—the situation was going to take some getting used to. He had a nice crib and a play area with plenty of appropriate toys for a young baby. When she'd put him down for his afternoon nap, she'd come straight in here and climbed into bed. She always tried to snatch a few moments' sleep while Nicky was out—but he usually woke her before she was fully rested.

A prickle of alarm began to grow in her belly as she reached for her cell phone. She blinked at the display, certain she wasn't seeing it right. Because, if she was, that meant she'd been asleep for nearly three hours now.

Holly scrambled off the bed and ran into the adjoining room. Panic slammed into her when she realized Nicky was not in the crib. She tore open the door and raced down the hall, skidding into the palatial living area, with its huge windows overlooking Central Park. A woman sat on the floor and played with her baby. Nicky was on his belly, twisting the knobs of a toy, and the woman made encouraging noises as he did so.

"Who are you?" Holly demanded. She was trembling as she stood there. Part of her wanted to snatch her baby up and take him away from this woman, but the rational part told her not to alarm him when he was perfectly happy with what he was doing. And clearly safe and well.

The woman got to her feet and smiled. She was older, a bit plain, dressed in jeans and a T-shirt. She held out her hand. "I'm Sylvia. Mr. Di Navarra hired me to help with your son."

Holly's throat tightened painfully. She would *not* allow him to interfere. "I don't need help," she said. "He made a mistake."

Sylvia frowned. "I apologize, Miss Craig, but Mr. Di Navarra seems to think you do."

"I will speak to Mr. Di Navarra," she said tightly.

"Speak to me about what?"

Holly spun to find Drago standing in the door. Her heart did that little skip thing she wished it wouldn't do at the sight of him. But he was beautiful, as always, and she couldn't help herself. How had this splendid creature ever been interested in her for even a moment? How had they managed to make a baby together when she was so clearly not the class of woman he was accustomed to?

He wore faded jeans that she knew were artfully faded rather than work faded, and a dark shirt that molded to the broad muscles of his chest. His feet were bare. Something about that detail made her heart skitter wildly.

"I don't need help to take care of my son," she said. "You've wasted this woman's time."

He came into the room then and she saw he was holding a newspaper at his side. He tossed it onto a table and kept walking.

"I beg your pardon." He was all arrogance and disdain once more. "But you definitely do."

He stopped in front of her and put two fingers under her chin. She flinched. And then he turned her head gently this way and that, his eyes raking over her.

"I intend to pay a lot of money for this face to grace my ads. I'd prefer if you truly are rested instead of having you edited to look that way."

She pulled out of his grip and glared at him. Of course he was concerned about the campaign. What had she expected? That he'd hired a nanny because he cared? He didn't care. He had never cared.

Strike that: he only cared about himself.

"You could have asked me. I didn't appreciate waking up and finding my baby gone."

"My mistake, then," he said, his eyes searching hers. "I told Sylvia to take him when he cried. I knew you didn't get enough sleep last night."

Holly didn't dare think the fact he'd noticed she didn't get enough sleep meant anything other than he wanted to protect his investment. But she couldn't remember the last time someone had paid attention to how much sleep she was getting. It made a lump form in her throat. Gabi would have noticed if she weren't in the same boat.

Gran would have, too. Gran would have put her to bed and taken the baby for as long as she needed. Holly bit the inside of her lip to stop a little sob from escaping. It wasn't even eighteen months since Gran had died, and it still hurt her at the oddest times.

Holly glanced at Sylvia, who had gotten back down on the floor to entice Nicky with a new toy. There was a tightness in her chest as she watched her baby play. She'd greatly appreciated Mrs. Turner's help, and she was certain the woman was kind and gentle, but she was almost positive Mrs. Turner had spent her time watching television instead of playing on the floor with Nicky.

Sylvia clearly knew what she was doing—in fact, Holly thought sadly, the woman seemed to know more than she did, if the way she encouraged Nicky to play with different shapes was any indication. Holly had been satisfied when he'd been occupied and happy. She'd never really considered his play to be a teaching moment.

Holly put a hand to her forehead and drew in a deep breath. She wasn't a bad mother, was she? She was simply an overworked and exhausted one, but she loved her son beyond reason. He was the only thing of value she had.

"You need to eat," Drago said, and Holly looked up at him.

"I'm not hungry." As if to prove her a liar, her stomach growled. Drago arched an eyebrow. "Fine," she said, "I guess I am after all."

"Come to the kitchen and let the cook fix you something."

Holly looked doubtfully at her baby and Sylvia. It wasn't that she didn't trust the woman, but she didn't know her. And she was nervous, she had to admit, with this change in circumstances. The last time she'd been here, it had all been ripped away from her without warning. She wasn't certain it wouldn't be again. "I'd rather stay here."

Drago frowned. "He's not going anywhere, Holly. He'll be perfectly fine."

Holly closed her eyes. She was being unreasonable. She'd left Nicky with Mrs. Turner for hours while she rode a bus and a streetcar halfway across town and went to work. Was it really such a stretch to go into another room and leave this woman alone with her child?

"All right," she said. Drago led her not to the kitchen but to a rooftop terrace with tables and chairs and grass—actual grass on a rooftop in New York City. The terrace was lined with potted trees and blossoming flowers, and while she could hear the city sounds below, her view was entirely of sky and plants and the buildings across the tree-tops in Central Park. Astounding, and beautiful in a way she found surprising.

"This is not the kitchen," she said inanely.

Drago laughed. "No. I decided this was more appropriate."

They sat down and a maid appeared with a tray laden with small appetizers—olives, sliced meats, tiny pastries filled with cheese, cucumber sandwiches, ham sandwiches and delicate chocolates to finish. It wasn't much, but it was precisely the kind of thing she needed just now.

Holly dug in to the food, filling her plate and taking careful bites so as not to seem like a ravenous animal. She might not be accustomed to fancy New York society, but her grandmother had at least taught her the art of being graceful. The maid appeared again with a bottle of wine. Holly started to protest, but Drago shushed her. Then he poured the beautiful deep red liquid into two glasses.

"You should appreciate this," he said. "A Château Margaux of excellent vintage."

As if she even knew what that meant. But she did understand scents and flavors. Holly lifted the wine and swirled it before sniffing the bowl. The wine was rich and full and delicious to the nose. She took a sip, expecting perfection. It was there. And she knew, as she set the glass down again, it was the sort of thing she could never afford.

When she glanced up, Drago was watching her. His gray eyes were piercing, assessing, and she met them evenly. So unlike the Holly of a year ago, who'd stammered and gulped and been a nervous wreck in his presence. It took a lot to meet that stare and not fold, but she was getting better at it.

"Describe the wine to me," he said, his voice smooth and commanding. As if he were accustomed to telling people what to do and then having them do it. Which, of course, he was.

Holly bristled, though it was a simple request. She was tired and stressed and not in the mood to play games with him. Not in the mood to be devoured like a frightened rabbit.

"Taste it yourself," she said. "I'm sure you can figure it out."

She didn't expect him to laugh. "You have made it your mission in life to argue with me, it seems."

"I wouldn't say it's a mission, as that implies I give you a lot of thought. But I'm not quite the same person you ordered around last year. I won't pretend I am."

She was still more of that person than she wanted to be, but she was working very hard on being bold and brave. On not letting his overwhelming force of a personality dominate her will.

Not that he needed to know that.

He leaned back and sipped his wine. "I didn't force you to do anything you didn't want to do, Holly. As I recall, you wanted to do the same things I did. Very much, in fact."

Holly tried to suppress the heat flaring in her cheeks. Impossible, of course. They were red and he would know it. "The wine is delicious," she said, picking up the glass and studying the color. "The top notes are blackberry and cassis. The middle might be rose, while the bottom hints at oak and coffee." A small furrow appeared between Drago's brows.

"Ah, you are embarrassed by what happened between us," he said softly.

Her heart skipped a beat. "Embarrassed? No. But I see no need in discussing it. It's in the past and I'd like to just forget the whole thing."

As if she could.

His nostrils flared, as if he didn't quite like that pronouncement. "Forget? Why would you want to forget something so magnificent, Holly?"

She picked up the wine and took another sip, kept her eyes on the red liquid instead of on him. "Why not? You did. You refused to listen to me and threw me out. I'm sure you promptly forgot about me once I was gone."

His handsome face creased in a frown. "That doesn't mean I didn't enjoy our evening together."

"I really don't want to talk about this," she said. Because it hurt, and because it made her think of her innocent child in the other room and the fact that his father sat here with her now and didn't even know it. Hadn't managed to even consider the possibility.

No, he thought she'd spent the night with him in order to sell her fragrances. And then, when that didn't work, he thought she'd run home and got pregnant right after. As if she had the sense of a goat and the morals of an alley cat.

Yes, she could tell him the truth…but she didn't know him, didn't trust him. And Nicky was too precious to her to take that kind of chance with.

"What you see here is not who I have always been," he

said, spreading an arm to encompass the roof with its expensive greenery. "It may appear as if I were born with money, but I assure you I was not. I know what it's like to work hard, and what it's like to want something so badly you'd sell your soul for it. I've seen it again and again."

Holly licked suddenly dry lips. Was he actually sharing something with her? Something important? Or was he simply trying to intimidate her in another way? "But Navarra Cosmetics has been around for over fifty years," she said. "You are a Navarra."

He studied the wine in his glass. "Yes, I am a Navarra. That doesn't mean I was born with a silver spoon, as you Americans say. Far from it." He drew in a breath. "But I'm here now, and this is my life. And I do not appreciate those who try to take advantage of who I am for their own ends."

Holly's heart hardened. She knew what he was saying. What he meant. Her body began to tremble. She wanted to tell him how wrong he was. How blind. But, instead, she pushed her chair back and stood. She couldn't take another moment of his company, another moment of his smugness.

"I think I'm finished," she said, disappointment and fury thrashing together inside her.

Of course he wasn't telling her anything important. He was warning her. Maybe he hadn't been born rich, maybe he'd been adopted or something, but she didn't care. He was still a heartless bastard with a supreme sense of arrogance and self-importance. He could only see what he expected to see.

If she didn't need the money so much, she'd walk out on *him*. Let him be the one to suffer—not that he would suffer much if she didn't do the Sky campaign. He'd find another model, like he had last year, and he'd eventually give up the idea of her being the right person for the job.

No, the only one who would suffer if she walked out was Nicky. She wasn't walking out. But she wasn't putting up with this, either. She was going back inside and collecting her baby. Then she was going to her room and staying there for the evening.

Before she could walk away, Drago reached out and encircled her wrist with his strong fingers. They sizzled into her, sending sparks of molten heat to her core. Her body ached when he touched her, and it made her angry. Why hadn't she ached when Colin had touched her? Why hadn't she wanted him the way she wanted Drago di Navarra?

Life would be so much easier if she had. Lisa Tate would have never entered the picture. Nicky might be Colin's son, and they might be married and living in her cottage in New Hope while he worked his lawn-care business and she made perfume for the little shop she'd always wanted to open.

They could have been a happy little family and life could have been perfect. She might have never gotten a chance to sell her fragrances to a big company, but Gran would have understood. Gran had only ever wanted her to be happy. She knew that now. A year ago, she'd thought she had to succeed in order to carry on Gran's legacy. That Gran was counting on her somehow.

But she knew Gran wouldn't have wanted her to suffer. She wouldn't have wanted Holly to work so hard, to scrape and scrape and barely get by. She'd have wanted Holly happy, living in their cottage and making her perfumes.

Except that living in the cottage hadn't been an option, had it? Gran's health had suffered in the last few years and she'd had to borrow against the house to pay her bills. Holly had hoped to save the only home she'd ever known when she'd gone to New York.

What a fool she'd been. She'd left the big city broke and pregnant and alone.

"So long as we know where we stand, there's no need to get upset," Drago said, his voice smooth and silky and hateful to her all at once. "Sit. Finish eating. You'll need your strength for the coming days. I can't afford for you to get sick on me."

Her wrist burned in his grip. She wanted to pull away. And she wanted to slide into his lap and wrap her arms around his proud neck. Holly blinked. Was she insane? Had she learned absolutely nothing about this man?

She hated him. Despised him.

Wanted him.

Impossible. Wanting him was a threat to her well-being. To her baby's well-being.

Holly closed her eyes and stood there, gathering her strength. She would need every bit of it to resist his touch. So long as he didn't touch her, she could remain aloof. She could remember the hate. Feel it. Soak in it. That was how she would survive this. By remembering how it had felt when he'd kicked her out. How she'd felt when she'd lost everything and given birth with only Gabi and the medical staff for company.

There'd been no happy new father, no roses, no balloons for the baby. No joy, other than what she'd felt when she'd held Nicky.

"I am finished," she said coolly. "And I'd appreciate it if you'd let go of me."

Drago's jaw was tight. He looked as if he were assessing her. Cataloging her flaws and finding her lacking, no doubt. "Sit down, Holly. We have much to discuss."

"I'd rather not right now, thanks."

His grip tightened on her wrist. Then he let her go abruptly, cursing in Italian as he did so. "Go, then. Run away like a child. But we will have a discussion about what I want from you. And quite soon."

Holly gritted her teeth together and stared across the beautiful terrace to the sliding-glass doors. Freedom was almost hers. All she had to do was walk away. Just go and get Nicky and go to her room for the night.

But it was simply postponing the inevitable. She knew that. It was what she wanted to do, and yet she couldn't. She had to face this head-on. Had to fight for this opportunity before he changed his mind.

Holly Craig wanted to be the kind of woman who didn't back down.

She *would* be that kind of woman. She sank down in her chair like a queen and crossed her legs, in spite of her racing heart. Then she picked up the still-full wineglass and leveled a gaze at Drago.

"Fine. Talk. I'm listening."

CHAPTER SIX

DRAGO HAD NEVER met a more infuriating woman in his life. Holly Craig sat across from him at the table, with golden sunlight playing across her face and her pale hair, setting flame to the strands, and looked like a sweet, innocent goddess.

An illusion.

She was not sweet. She was most definitely not innocent. Remembering the ways in which she was not innocent threatened to make him hard, especially after he'd just had his hand on her soft skin. He forced the memory of making love to her from his mind and focused on the stubborn set of her jaw.

So determined, this woman. So different compared to last year. He sometimes had glimpses of that innocent girl under the veneer, but mostly she was hard and weary. Changed.

Or perhaps last year had been nothing more than an act. Perhaps she'd been just as hard then but had pretended not to be. He'd learned, over the years, that women would do much in an attempt to snare a wealthy man. Holly might have been a virgin, but that didn't mean she hadn't been a virgin with a plan. Innocence in sexual matters did not imply innocence overall.

Nevertheless, he still wanted her for Sky. She had the face he needed. An everywoman face, but pretty in the way every woman wanted to be. No, she was not perfect. She wasn't the sort of gorgeous that a top supermodel was.

But she was perfect for what he wanted her for.

And that was why he put up with her, he told himself. With her hostility and her loathing and her refusal to co-operate.

Drago had worked his way up the ladder at Navarra Cosmetics, because his uncle had insisted he start at the bottom to really know the business, but one of the things he'd always had—and had honed into a fine instrument these days—was a gut feeling for what was right for the company. Holly Craig was right for Sky, and he intended to have her.

Even if he had to suffer her hostility and a baby in his house. When they went to Italy, he would put her and the child in another wing of the estate. Then he would cheerfully forget about her until the shoot was completed and he went over the photos.

She took a sip of the wine and he thought of the way she'd described it to him. She'd never had Château Margaux, he'd bet on that, but she'd described it perfectly after one sip. She knew scents and flavors, he had to give her that.

Whether or not that made her a good perfumer was an entirely different matter.

"Tell me what you expected when you came to New York last year."

Her eyes widened. And then narrowed again, as if she were trying to figure out the trick.

"I'm not sure what you mean," she said carefully.

Her eyes dropped and a current of irritation sizzled into him. "Are you not? You had a case of perfume samples. You pretended to be a model. What was your intent? What did you think would happen once you had my undivided attention?"

She colored, her eyes flashing hot. He didn't know why, but that slice of temper intrigued him. "Because I had intent, right? You never gave me a chance to explain that morning, if I recall. It was a misunderstanding, but you didn't stay for that part."

He sipped the wine. "How did I misunderstand you, *cara*? You were not mute. You spent the entire evening with me. Not only that, but you stood in front of the cameras for two hours and never corrected the impression you were there to model."

Her color remained high. She closed her eyes for a moment. A second later, she was looking straight at him, her eyes shiny and big in her pale face. "I know. I should have. But you assumed I was a model, and I was too scared to say otherwise. Scared I'd lose my chance to talk to you."

"You had my undivided attention all evening," he bit out.

"Hardly undivided," she threw back at him. "You took a dozen phone calls at least. How anyone could have a conversation with you under those circumstances is beyond me."

"Ah, so this is your excuse. What about later, *cara*?"

He didn't think it possible, but her color heightened. Her cheeks were blazing now. She picked up her untouched glass of water and took a deep draft. Drago almost wanted to laugh, but he was too irritated. Still, her blushes made him think of how inexperienced she'd been——and how eager at the same time.

Basta, no. Not a good thing to think about.

"We were, um, busy later. I didn't think it was appropriate." Her head came up then and her eyes glittered. "Haven't you ever stopped to wonder how I could have possibly known you needed a model that day? How I just happened to be sitting there in your waiting room? It wasn't planned, Drago. I had an appointment." She cleared her throat. "Or I thought I did. A university friend of the mayor's wife said she knew you and could arrange a brief meeting. I was told the day and time and that I would have ten minutes. So I went."

It could be true, certainly. He had no recollection. But that did not change what she'd done. How she'd lied. "And yet you took advantage of the situation when I mistook you for the model."

She let out an exasperated breath. "I did. I admit it! But you ordered me to go with you and you didn't give me a chance to explain. I made a decision that it was best to go along with you until I could."

Drago studied her for a long moment. Did he really believe Holly Craig had masterminded the entire situation?

No, he didn't. But she had taken advantage of it. Of him. And that was unforgivable.

"It's possible you were on the schedule. But that was a bad day, as I recall. All the models were wrong. I told my secretary to reschedule the meetings."

She looked unhappy. "Since I didn't schedule it, it wasn't my contact information she would have had. Besides, I'd already come all that way. I couldn't go back without talking to you."

Yes, and she'd been sitting there in his waiting room, looking so fresh and out of place at the same time. He still remembered the black suit and the pink heels with the price tag. A twinge of something sliced into him, but he didn't want to examine it. And he definitely wasn't revisiting what had happened next. It might have been a mistake, but she'd had ample opportunity to tell him the truth.

Instead, she'd seen a way to gain advantage—and she'd taken it. Then she'd kept the pretense going until she'd thought she had him right where she wanted him. He could still see her face that morning, still see how pleased she'd been with herself when he'd questioned her about the case.

His reaction had been inevitable. He'd experienced all those old feelings of despair and fear and loneliness he'd had as a boy, and he'd hated her for doing that to him. For making him remember what he'd worked hard to bury. He'd had no choice but to walk out.

Because she'd blindsided him and he hadn't seen it coming. He'd thought she was someone she wasn't, and he'd felt something with her that he hadn't felt in a long time. He had almost—almost, but not quite—let himself relax with her. She'd been so guileless, unlike the women he usually dated. His fault for always choosing sophisticates, but until he'd experienced someone like Holly Craig, he'd not realized he might enjoy less artifice.

That she'd fooled him, that she'd been as scheming as the most seasoned gold digger, still rankled. He did not regret throwing her out.

But he did regret that he'd let her escape without first seeing the photos. He'd thought about tracking her down once she was gone, but he'd ultimately decided it was best if he did not.

"And what did you hope to gain from a meeting with me? A job?"

She shook her head. "I had hoped you would want Colette."

"Colette?"

"It's named after my grandmother. It's the last fragrance we created together. The finest, I might add. I had hoped you would buy it and market it."

"Surely you know this is not how huge companies work." He slid his fingers along the stem of his wineglass. "At Navarra, we employ several perfumers. We brainstorm concepts and give directions. The perfumers work to create something that meets our expectations. Sometimes, we create fragrances in tandem with celebrities. We do not, however, buy fragrances from individuals."

Her chin lifted. "Yes, but this one is good enough you might have. And I had to try."

He could almost admire her determination. Almost. "Why?"

She turned her head and put her fingers to her lips. He wondered if she was thinking about her answer, but when she turned back to him, he could see the sheen of moisture in her eyes. "Because my gran was gone and I didn't want to lose her house. I wanted to honor her memory and save my childhood home at the same time."

Inside, a tiny flicker of unease reared its head. "And did you lose the house?" He knew the answer because of how he'd found her. If she'd still had her childhood home, would she have been a cocktail waitress in a casino? Especially with a baby?

There were two fresh spots of color in her cheeks. "I did. I couldn't make the payments against the debt, so it was sold. A nice couple lives there now."

He hadn't had a childhood home. The thought made him feel raw inside. But he'd wanted one. He'd been eleven when his uncle had finally wrested him from his mother's capricious grip. Eleven when he'd first entered the Di Navarra estate in Tuscany. It was as close to a childhood home as he had.

Except, he had no memories of a mother's love or of warmth and belonging in a place. His uncle had been good to him, and he was grateful, but he'd spent a lot of time alone—or with tutors—because Uncle Paolo had spent so much time working.

"Where are your parents?" he asked her.

"I never knew them. My father is a mystery man, and my mother died when I was a baby." She said it so unemotionally, but he knew it had to hurt. He'd never known his father, though of course he knew his identity. He hadn't been that lucky with his mother. She had left her imprint deep. He was still trying to cover the scars of what she'd done to him.

"And what about the father of your child?" he asked, shaking away painful thoughts of his mother. "Why didn't he step up and help?"

Her lips flattened and she took a deep breath. "He didn't want to be burdened, I imagine," she finally said, her voice soft and brittle at once.

He imagined her pregnant and alone, without a home, and felt both anger and sympathy. Anger because she reminded him of his mother and sympathy because she'd lost so much. Was that what had happened to his mother? He'd never understood why she'd been so flighty, why she'd moved from place to place, always searching for something that eluded her.

She might have had to settle down if not for him. If not for the money he represented. The money his uncle gave for his care, but which she would spend taking him someplace remote and hiding him from the Di Navarras. When she would run out, she would emerge again, hand outstretched until Uncle Paolo filled it—and then they would disappear once more.

Clearly, Holly wasn't doing that with this child—but she had been living in that dingy building and leaving the baby with strangers. His mother had done the same thing, time and again. If Holly got money from the baby's father, would she spend it all recklessly in the pursuit of filling some emptiness inside herself? Or would she settle down and take care of the baby the way he should be taken care of?

"I am given to understand you can sue for child support in this country," he said mildly. "At the least, you could have gotten a bit of help for your child. I wonder that you did not do it."

Her eyes flashed hot. "You make it sound so simple.

But I would have needed money for a lawyer, wouldn't I? Since I couldn't afford to make the mortgage payments, I couldn't afford a lawyer, either."

"So you got a job as a cocktail waitress." There was condemnation in his tone. He knew it, and so did she. Certainly she could have found something else. Something safer for a child.

Her chin came up. "After I left New Hope, yes. I went to New Orleans and got a job in the casino. The tips were good and I needed the money."

"But not good enough to afford you a decent place to live."

"Not everyone is so fortunate as you."

"I have had nothing handed to me, *cara*. I worked for everything I have."

"Yes, but you had all the advantages."

"Not quite all," he said. For the first eleven years, he'd had no advantages. Hell, he hadn't even been able to read until Uncle Paolo had taken him away from his mother and gotten him an education that didn't require him to count out coins for supper. "Besides, when you are done here, you'll have enough money to take your baby somewhere safe."

"How dare you suggest I would put my baby in danger?" she said tightly. "Just because I couldn't afford a home that meets *your* standards, Your High and Mightiness, doesn't mean my son wasn't safe."

She was tightly strung, her body practically trembling with nervous energy. Her eyes flashed fire and her jaw was set in that stubborn angle he'd oddly come to enjoy. Such a firecracker, this girl.

They'd burned together before. What would it be like now?

He shoved the thought away and let his gaze slide over

her lovely face. She was going to make Navarra Cosmetics a lot of money, if his gut was any judge. And it usually was.

He didn't need to screw it up by getting involved with her again, however enticing the thought. Instead, he thought of where he'd found her, of the utter desolation of that apartment building, and his anger whipped higher.

"Do you really want your child to grow up there, Holly? Do you want Mrs. Turner keeping him every night, while he cries and asks where his mother is? Do you want him to only see you for a few minutes a day while you do whatever it is you plan to do with the money?"

She blinked at him, and he knew his voice had grown harsh. But he wouldn't take any of it back. She had to consider these things. She had to consider the child.

"Of course I don't want that," she said. "I want a house somewhere, and a good school. I want Nicky to have everything I had growing up. I intend to give it to him, too."

Everything inside him was tight, as if someone had stretched the thinnest membrane over the mouth of a volcano. He didn't know why she got to him so badly, but he didn't like it. Drago worked to push all the feelings she'd whipped up back under the lid of the box he kept them in.

"Perhaps you can give him those things," he finally said when he no longer felt so volatile. "Do you have any idea what the going rate is on a cosmetics campaign?"

She shook her head.

"It could be in the six figures, *cara*. But we'll need to see how the test shots go first." Because, no matter how bad he felt for her and the baby, he wouldn't hand over that kind of money for nothing. He'd go out of business if he allowed sympathy to get in the way of his decisions.

Her eyes were huge. Then she swallowed and fixed him with a determined look. "I expect to see that contract, spelling it all out, before anything happens."

Irritation lashed into him. "You don't trust me?" he asked, a dangerous edge to his voice.

She was nobody. She had nothing. She needed this job—and she needed his goodwill, after what she'd pulled last year.

But she didn't hesitate to push him. To demand her contract. He had to admit that a grudging part of him admired her tenacity even while she maddened him.

"Should I?" she said sweetly.

"Do you have a choice?"

Her jaw worked. Hardened. "No, I don't suppose I do."

"Precisely." He shoved back from the table and stood. "You will get your contract, Holly, because that is what businesses do."

Then he leaned down, both hands on the table, and fixed her with an even look. "And if you don't like the terms, you will be taken back to where I found you and left there without the possibility of ever seeing a dime."

Holly was restless. She was so accustomed to being on the go, to working hard for hours every day and then scrambling to get home and take care of her child, that being in this apartment with a nanny and no schedule felt surreal.

She'd tried to read a book. She'd tried to watch television—what was with all these people airing their private business in front of a TV judge for public consumption, anyway?—and she'd tried to listen to music. Nothing made her feel settled for more than a few moments.

She thought about going for a walk, but she was a little too intimidated by the prospect of roaming New York City streets alone. She'd walked the short distance from the casino to the streetcar stop in the dark—risky enough in some ways, but she'd never felt intimidated doing it.

Here, she thought if she went outside, she might never find her way back again.

So, she sat with the television remote and skipped through a variety of shows. And she finally had to admit to herself that the source of her restlessness wasn't just that her life had gone from two hundred miles an hour to a full stop in the space of a heartbeat.

No, it was also Drago di Navarra. He'd been angry at her earlier, and he'd threatened to drop her back in New Orleans, where he'd found her. The thought had chilled her. Yes, she was murderously furious with him—with his high-handedness and his arrogance and his certainty she'd been out to dupe him—but she couldn't let her anger get in the way of this job. She couldn't let him send her away before she'd earned that money.

It frightened her that she was suddenly so dependent on the promise of so much money. Yesterday, she'd nearly thrown a tray of drinks in his face. She'd been hostile to him and she'd wanted him gone—but he'd seduced her with words, with the promise of a better life for her child, and now she'd bought into it so thoroughly that the prospect of not having it threatened to make her physically ill.

She'd pushed him during their conversation. She'd been angry and she'd lashed out. Part of her regretted it—and part of her was glad. Damn him and his smug superiority anyway!

As if thinking of the devil conjured him, Drago walked into the living room, dressed in a tuxedo and looking every inch the gorgeous tycoon. Holly's heart thumped. Her jaw sagged and she snapped it closed again when she realized she was gaping at him.

Of course he was going out. Of course.

She didn't know where he was going, or who he was going with, but the thought of him out there dancing with some beautiful woman pierced her.

Why?

She did not care what he did. Holly lifted her chin and

stared at him, waiting for him to speak. Because, clearly, he'd come in here to say something to her. Perhaps he'd decided she wasn't worth the trouble after all. Perhaps he'd come to tell her to gather her things because a car was waiting to take her back to the airport.

"I have to go out," he said without preamble, and she let her gaze drop over him.

"I can see that. Have a wonderful time."

He ignored her and came over to perch on the arm of the chair facing where she sat. The TV was behind him, so she tried to focus on it.

Impossible, of course.

"We need to talk," he said, and her heart skipped. He was going to send her home. It was over. Well, she'd known it couldn't last. But he was going to have to pay her for her inconvenience, damn him. She'd left her job, for heaven's sake.

He lifted his arm, tugged the cuff of his sleeve. Adjusting. Making her wait for it. He was so cool, so unconcerned. His gaze lifted, bored into hers.

"Do you have a passport?" he asked, and Holly blinked.

"I— Um, no." Well, that wasn't what she'd expected.

He frowned. "Then we'll need to take care of it. As soon as possible."

"Why?"

"Because we are going to Italy, *cara*."

Italy? Her pulse throbbed with a sudden shot of fear. "Why?"

He looked annoyed. "Because this is where the Sky shoot will take place. Because I am the boss and I say so."

Holly shifted on the couch. "You aren't my boss," she pointed out, and then berated herself for doing so. But why should she let him get away with being so pointedly arrogant? He'd asked her to do the campaign. She'd said yes— but they hadn't started yet and she didn't have a contract.

He lifted one eyebrow. "Am I not? Somehow, I thought the one paying the salary would be in charge."

"You haven't paid me a single penny yet," she said.

"Haven't I? You did not get to New York by magic, Holly. Nor does Sylvia work for free."

Her ears felt hot. Well, yes, those things did cost money. "I did not ask you to hire her."

"No, but a baby on the hip was not quite what I had in mind for the ad."

"I won't go to Italy without a contract." She said it belligerently, and then winced at her tone. What was the matter with her? Did she want him to send her home? Back to nothing?

"These things take time to draft," he said coolly. "I don't keep a sheaf of contracts in my desk and whip one out as needed. Rest assured, Holly, you will get a contract. But you still need a passport, and so does the baby."

Her heart slid into her stomach. She'd never filled out paperwork for a passport before, but she imagined it required information she'd rather not share with Drago. Information that might make him ask questions.

"I don't understand why we can't do the shoot here. We did before. The park is lovely, and—"

"Because it's not what I want this time," he said. "Because I have a vision, and that vision takes place in Italy."

She dropped her gaze to the tips of her tennis shoes, where they rested on the ottoman in front of her. Jeez, he sat there in a tuxedo, and she was wearing jeans and tennis shoes as if she was still a teenager or something.

It reminded her starkly of the difference in their circumstances.

"It seems like a waste of money," she said softly. "The park is here, and it was so pretty the last time."

He stood and she could feel his imposing gaze on her. She looked up, and her heart turned over at the intensity of his stare. There was something in that gray-eyed gaze, something hot and secret and compelling.

Holly swallowed.

"I appreciate you thinking about the bottom line," he said with only the mildest hint of sarcasm, "but the fact is I can afford to do what I want. And what I want is you in Italy."

Holly twisted her fingers together in her lap. "Then I suppose we'll have to get passports."

"Yes," he said. "You shall. I'll make arrangements." He looked at his watch and frowned. "And now, if you will excuse me, I have a date."

A date.

Holly's stomach twisted, but she forced herself to give him a wan smile. Really, she didn't care at all—but being here made her remember what it had been like between them. The heat and passion and pleasure, the utter bliss of his possession.

Another woman would experience that tonight, while Holly lay in a bed in his apartment, only steps from the room where he'd first shown her what it was like between a man and a woman. She would twist and turn and imagine him with someone else. She would burn with longing, the way she'd done during the lonely nights when she hadn't been able to stop thinking about him no matter how much she'd wanted to.

Holly picked up the remote and flipped through the channels. She didn't see what was on the screen, couldn't have focused if her life depended on it, but it was something to do while she waited for him to walk out.

"Have fun," she said, because she had to say something.

He stood there a moment more, hands thrust in pockets. And then he turned and walked out and her heart slid to the bottom of her toes. Her eyes stung with unshed tears that she angrily slapped away.

She was furious because she was helpless. Because she had to do what he wanted or lose the money. That was the reason she wanted to cry.

The *only* reason.

Drago was not enjoying himself. He'd been expected to attend this event for the past month—a charity gala at the Met—but his attention was elsewhere. The woman on his arm—a beautiful heiress he'd met at a recent business dinner—bored him. He didn't remember her boring him when he'd met her only a few weeks ago. He remembered that he'd been interested.

She was lovely and articulate, and she had her fingers in many causes. But he saw beneath that veneer tonight. She had causes because she needed something to do with her money and her time.

She didn't care about the people she helped. She did it because it was expected of her. And because it brought her attention. He remembered seeing her in the paper only a couple of days ago, being interviewed about some fashion show she'd attended in Europe.

Even that wouldn't have been enough to make him think she didn't really care. No, it was her behavior tonight. Her need to be seen on his arm and her ongoing *catty* chatter about some of the other people in the room. As if she were better than them. As if he were, too, and needed to be warned about them.

The disconcerting thing was this: he wasn't quite certain any of these things would have truly bothered him just a few days ago. But now he thought of Holly sitting in that squalid apartment and feeding her baby a bottle, and a hot feeling bloomed in his chest.

Holly knew what it was like to struggle. To have almost nothing. She'd lost her home, and she'd gone to work as a waitress to make ends meet. His mother had done much the same, though for reasons of her own that had made no sense to anyone but her.

This woman—Danielle, was it?—wouldn't know the first thing about what struggling really meant.

He did. Even if he hadn't been a part of that world in a very long time, he knew what it was to have nothing. To rely on the kindness of strangers to eat. To beg and struggle and do things you didn't want to do, simply because you needed to survive. He'd only been a child, but the memory was imprinted deep. It was also usually buried deep—but not since Holly Craig had come back into his life.

"Drago, did you hear anything I said?"

He looked down at the glittering creature by his side—and a wave of disgust filled him. He didn't want this artifice. Not tonight. He didn't want to spend his time in the company of a woman who was superficial and selfish. She had millions, but she was still a user. A user of a different kind than his mother had been, but a user nonetheless. It dismayed him that he'd never seen it before.

Tonight, he wanted a woman who would look at him like he wasn't a god, a woman who would refuse to accept his pronouncements as if they were from some exalted place and, therefore, not to be questioned.

He wanted Holly. He wanted a woman who was direct with him. Oh, she hadn't always been. But she was now. She knew where she stood with him, so she was no longer trying to scam him. There was no need for pretense between them. She glared and huffed and stubbornly tried to get her way. She did not cajole. She spoke her mind.

No one spoke their mind to him. Not the way Holly did. She didn't even seem to like him much—but she did want him.

He knew that from the way her breath shortened when he was near, the way her eyes slid over him and then quickly away, as if she didn't want to be caught looking at him. Her skin grew pink and her breathing shallow.

That wasn't hatred, no matter what she claimed. It was desire.

"I heard you," he said to the woman at his side. "And I am terribly sorry, but I have to leave. I'm afraid I have another engagement tonight."

Danielle's mouth opened, as if she couldn't quite believe it. "But I thought…"

Drago lifted her limp, cool hand to his mouth and pressed a kiss there. "*Ciao, bella.* It was lovely to see you again."

And then, before she could utter another word, he strode from her side, out the front doors and down the sidewalk. His apartment wasn't far. His driver would have come to pick him up, but he wanted to walk. He needed to walk if he were to quench this strange fire for Holly Craig, before he stormed into his home and took her into his arms.

It was inconvenient to want a woman he'd once thrown out of his life. But he couldn't seem to stop himself.

He reached his building in less than fifteen minutes. The doorman swung the entry open with a cheery good-evening. Drago returned the greeting, and then he was in his private elevator and on his way up to the penthouse.

It was quiet when he let himself in. He glanced at his watch. It wasn't late, only nine-thirty. But his apartment was just as always. There was no television blaring, no one sitting in the living room, no baby on the floor surrounded by toys.

He found that oddly disappointing. He didn't care much for babies, but when he'd walked in earlier and seen Sylvia playing with the child while Holly made up a bottle, he'd had an odd rush of warmth in his chest. He'd dismissed it as something minor; a physical malady like acid reflux.

But now he felt strangely hollow, as if that warmth

would rush back if Holly were here with her son. He strode through the living room and toward the hall where the bedrooms were, his heart pounding. What if she'd left? What if she'd changed her mind and taken her opportunity to leave while he was out?

He'd taken the precaution of informing his driver—and the doorman—to alert him if she did, but no one had called. So why did he feel anxious?

A sound came from the direction of the kitchen, and he stopped, his heart thumping steadily as his ears strained to hear it again. It was late enough that the staff he employed would have gone home for the day, so he didn't expect to find any of them lurking about the kitchen.

He stopped abruptly as his gaze landed on the figure of a woman standing at the counter, her long blond hair caught in a loose ponytail. She was wearing yoga pants and a baggy T-shirt that looked as if it had been washed so frequently the color had faded to a flat red, one shade removed from pink.

She reached up to open the microwave and took out a bowl of something. Then she set a baby bottle inside it. Something about watching her warm the bottle hit him square in the gut. He'd never considered his life to be lacking, never felt as if he were missing out by not having a wife and children. He didn't know how to be close to anyone, not really, and he didn't know how to bridge that gap.

He'd always been on the outside looking in. And it had never bothered him until this moment. It was not a pleasant sensation to feel like an outsider in his own house.

But he did. And it made him feel empty in a way he had not in a very long time.

CHAPTER SEVEN

SOME SIXTH SENSE told Holly she wasn't alone. The skin on the back of her neck prickled and heat gathered in her core. She knew who it was. She didn't have to see him to know. She could feel him. Smell him.

She turned slowly, nonchalantly, her heart pounding in her breast. The sight of him in that tuxedo nearly made her heart stop. He was dark, beautiful, his gray eyes heated and intense as he watched her. He looked…broody, as if he'd had a bad evening. As if something had gone awry.

Was it wrong that her heart soared to think his date might not have worked out?

"You're back early," she said, keeping her voice as even as she could. Hoping he didn't hear the little catch in her throat.

"Perhaps I am not," he said, moving toward her, all hot handsome male. His hands were in his pockets and his jacket was open to reveal the perfect line of studs holding his shirt closed. His bow tie was still tight, as if he were going to an event instead of coming from one. "How would you know which it is?"

Holly turned to check the bottle. Not quite ready yet, so she dropped it back in the water. Then she shrugged. "I wouldn't. I'm just guessing. You don't strike me as the 'home and in bed by ten o'clock' type."

The moment she said it, she wished she could call the

words back. Heat flared in her cheeks, her throat, at the mention of Drago and a bed. Good grief, what was the matter with her?

Drago arched one eyebrow, and she knew he wasn't about to let her get away with that statement without comment.

"Oh, I most definitely am the 'home and in bed' type. Sometimes, I like to skip the evening out and go straight to bed."

Holly deliberately pretended not to understand. "How tragic for you. I would have thought the rich and dynamic CEO of a major corporation dedicated to making people beautiful would like to see and be seen."

"There's a time for everything, *cara mia*," he said, his voice low and sexy and relentless in the way it made vibrations of pleasure move through her body.

She'd spent the past few hours thinking about him. Wondering what he was doing tonight, if he was waltzing under the stars with some beauty, captivating her the way he'd once captivated Holly. He was a mesmerizing man when he set his mind to it. It had depressed her to think of him turning his charm onto another woman.

She told herself the only reason for her feelings was because she was here, in his apartment again, where he'd made love to her and created a baby. Her feelings were only natural in this setting. They would abate as soon as she was gone from this place.

He came closer, until she could smell him. Until her senses were wrapped in Drago di Navarra and the cool, clean, expensive fragrance of him. It wasn't just his cologne, which was subtle as always. It was him. *His* fragrance.

She wanted to turn and press her cheek to his chest, wanted to slide her fingers along the satin of his lapels, and just pretend for a moment that he was hers.

"Yes, and now it's time to feed Nicky," she said, her voice trembling more than she would have liked as she checked the bottle again. It was almost ready, but not quite. She set it back in the water with shaking fingers and then turned to lean against the marble counter. "So tell me all about your evening. Was it fun? Did you see anybody cool?"

He blinked. "Anybody cool?"

"You know. A movie star or something."

He shrugged. "There might have been. I wasn't paying attention."

Holly could only shake her head. Drago was a law unto himself, a man unimpressed with such fickle things as fame. It would take a very great deal to impress him, she imagined.

"Oh, yes, I suppose these things are ever so tedious for you," she said, with more than a little sarcasm. "Dress up in expensive finery, drink champagne, eat fancy hors d'oeuvres and hobnob with celebrities. What a life."

"Actually," he said, "it is tedious sometimes. Especially when the people one is with are shallow and self-absorbed."

Holly wanted to say something about how he was shallow and self-absorbed, but she suddenly couldn't do it. She should, but she couldn't seem to make the words come out. Because, right now, he looked a little lost. A little bleak. She wasn't sure why, but from the moment she'd turned around and seen him there, she'd been thinking of a lost and lonely soul.

Completely incongruous, since Drago di Navarra didn't *have* a soul. She tried to call up her anger with him, but it wouldn't surface.

She shrugged. "There are shallow people everywhere. I could tell you tales about the casino, believe me."

His eyes were hot and sharp. "And then there are people like you."

Her heart sped up. She swallowed the sudden lump in her throat. "What does that mean?"

He came and put his hands on her shoulders, stunning her. A shiver slid down her spine, a long slow lazy glide that left flame in its wake. Her body knew the touch of his. Craved it.

Holly felt frantic. *No, no, no.* It had hurt too much the last time she'd let him touch her. Not during, but after. When he'd sent her away. When she'd known she would never see him again. When he'd shattered her stupid, innocent heart into a million pieces. She hadn't been in love with him—how could she have been in only one night?—but he'd made her feel special, wonderful, beautiful. And she'd mourned because his rejection meant she hadn't been any of those things.

She could not endure those feelings again.

"What do you think it means?" he asked.

Holly sucked in a breath as doubt and confusion ricocheted through her head. "I think it means you're trying to seduce me again."

He laughed, and warmth curled deep inside her. She loved his laugh. He seemed a different man when he laughed. More open and carefree. He was too guarded, too cold otherwise. She could like him when he laughed.

"*Dio*, you amuse me, *cara*. Perhaps I was too hasty last year."

She refused to let those words warm her or vindicate her. "Perhaps you were," she said shakily.

His hands moved up and down her arms. Gently, sensually. She wanted to moan with everything he made her feel. "And yet here we are, with an entire evening to kill."

His voice was heady, deep and dark, and it made her think of tangled limbs and satiny skin. Of pleasure so intense she must have surely exaggerated it in her mind. Nothing could be that good. Could it?

Holly dug her fingernails into her palms, reminding herself there was pain in his proposition. Because it hadn't ended well the last time, and she didn't expect it would end any better now. She could take no risks.

"I'm sorry, but it's too late, Drago. You lost your chance to make me your sex slave. I am slave to only one man now, and he's pint-size and ready for his bottle."

Drago let his hands slide down her arms before he dropped them to his sides. Perversely, it stung her pride that he accepted her pronouncement so easily. As if he hadn't really wanted her after all.

"He's lucky to have a mother so dedicated."

Holly's pulse thumped. She let her gaze drop as a wave of hot shame rolled through her. "I do my best. I could probably do better."

Drago put a finger under her chin and lifted her gaze to his. His eyes bored into hers. "What makes you say this, Holly?"

Tears sprang to life behind her eyes and she closed them briefly, forcing herself to push them down again. She would not cry. She would not show a single moment of vulnerability to this man. She had to protect herself. To do that, she had to be strong. Immovable.

She wasn't so good at that, but she was learning. She had no room for softness anymore. Not for anyone but her son.

"I've worked so much," she said, her voice hoarse. "I haven't always been there for him. I hated leaving him with a babysitter every day. And I hated where we lived, Drago, but it was the best I could do."

He sighed again. "Things could have been far worse, believe me. You did what you had to do."

She didn't like the look in his eyes just then. Bleak. Desolate. As if he knew firsthand what those worse things were.

"I did the best I could. We weren't homeless and we had enough to eat."

A dark look crossed his face, and her heart squeezed in her chest. She almost reached up, almost put her palm on his jaw and caressed it as she'd done once before so long ago. But he took a step backward and put distance between them again.

"And now you are doing better. Working for me will give you a fresh start, Holly. You'll have more options."

She let out a shaky breath. "That's why I'm here."

He was frowning. Holly gripped the counter behind her until her fingers ached from the effort. She suddenly wanted to go to him, slip her arms around his waist. The only thing stopping her was the stone in her hands, anchoring her.

"You should have demanded help from his father," Drago said tightly. "He shouldn't have let you struggle so hard."

A shiver rolled through her then, stained her with the unmistakable brush of guilt. Oh God. "I couldn't," she choked out. "H-he made himself unavailable."

Drago looked suddenly angry. "Is he married, Holly?"

She was too stunned to react. And then, before her brain had quite caught up to her reflexes, she nodded once, quickly. A voice inside her shrieked in outrage. What was she doing? Why was she lying? Why didn't she just tell him the truth?

He would understand. He'd just said he knew she'd done her best. He would help her now, he would be a father to their child—

No. She knew none of those things. He was so intense, so powerful, and she had no idea what he would do if she told him the truth. What if he didn't believe her? What if he threw her out again, before she could earn the first cent? She needed this money too badly to risk it. And she needed to protect her child.

Until she had the contract, that ironclad promise of money, she couldn't risk the truth. She had to protect Nicky. He came first.

Drago's gaze was hard and her heart turned over in her chest. It ached so much she thought she might crumple to the floor in agony.

Your fault, her inner voice said.

"I'm sorry if that disappoints you," she told him, her voice on the edge of breaking. She shouldn't care what he thought, but she found that she did.

His eyebrows rose. "Disappoints me?" He shook his head. "I wasn't thinking that at all, Holly. I was thinking what a bastard this man is for leaving you so vulnerable."

Oh, goodness. He looked fierce, angry, as if he would go to battle for her and Nicky right this moment. It made the guilt inside her that much deeper, that much thicker and harder to shake off. She could endure him better when he was arrogant and bossy. She couldn't endure his empathy.

"I didn't tell him," she blurted, and Drago's expression turned to one of surprise.

She dropped her gaze to the floor. Holy cow, she was digging herself a hole, wasn't she? A giant hole from which she'd never escape.

"Didn't tell him? You mean, this man has no idea he has a son?"

She nodded, her heart pounding. "I tried, b-but he wouldn't listen. He didn't want to know."

Drago looked stunned, as if that thought had never occurred to him, and the quicksand under her feet shifted faster. Blindly, she turned and reached for the bottle. She couldn't stand here another minute. Couldn't sink deeper into the mire of lies and half-truths.

"I have to go feed Nicky."

She started to bolt from the room, but Drago's hand on her elbow caught her up short. "It's not too late to make this man meet his obligations—"

"It is," she said sharply. "It just is."

Drago sat at his desk and thought of Holly's face when she'd told him about the father of her baby the night before. She'd seemed so ashamed, so vulnerable. He'd wanted to pull her into his arms and tell her it was all right. Tell her she didn't need to worry. He'd considered, briefly, finding this man and forcing him to acknowledge his child.

But Holly's reaction told him everything he needed to know. She was scared of this man, whoever he might be. And as much as that angered him, as much as it made him want to find the bastard and thrash him for hurting her, Drago wasn't going to press the issue.

Besides, if this man came forward, there'd be someone else in Holly's life. Someone besides him. He wasn't quite sure why that thought bothered him, but it did. He didn't want to share her with another man.

Drago closed his eyes and pulled in a deep breath. No, it wasn't that he didn't want to share her. What an absurd thought. They'd had a hot night together, a fabulous night, but she had a baby now and he didn't see himself getting involved with a woman who had a baby.

The idea was fraught with pitfalls. Yes, he'd certainly like to have sex with her again. He wanted to take her to his bed and see if it was as good as he remembered.

But he couldn't. She'd shown him a vulnerability last night that had sliced into his chest and wrapped around his heart. She'd been frightened and confused—and worried. He didn't want or need that kind of intimacy. He wanted the physical without the emotional—and Holly Craig wasn't capable of that right now.

Drago ran both hands through his hair and turned to stare out across the city. He loved the city, loved the hustle and bustle, the sense of life that permeated the streets every hour of every day. New York City truly was the city that never slept.

But, right now, he wanted to be somewhere that slept. He wanted to be somewhere quieter, where life was more still. He wanted to take Holly and her infant to Italy.

But if he were going to get her to Italy, he had to get the passports taken care of. Drago opened an email from his secretary, who had informed him of what they would need to expedite the process. He made notes of what was required and went on to the next email.

This one contained sales figures for the quarter. Navarra Cosmetics was doing fabulously, thanks to a new skin-care line aimed at the middle-aged consumer. They had also debuted a new palette of colors for eyes, lips and cheeks that was doing quite well.

The numbers on fragrances were good. But Sky wasn't doing quite as well as he wanted for the new signature fragrance. Other CEOs would be perfectly happy with these numbers. But he wasn't. Because he *knew* they could be better.

Drago sat there a moment longer, thinking. And then he logged off his computer and informed his secretary he was leaving for the day. How could he concentrate when he was eager to revamp the Sky campaign? In order to do that, he needed passports for Holly and her child.

By the time Drago walked into his apartment, nearly half an hour later, he was no closer to understanding this strange pull Holly Craig had on him or why he was taking off in the middle of the day to do something he could have sent any number of assistants to do.

But when he strode into the living room and saw her on the floor with her baby, he got that same strange rush of warmth he'd had the first time. She looked up, her eyes wide and wounded, and his chest felt tight.

"*Ciao,* Holly," he said, dropping his briefcase on a nearby table.

She smiled, but it didn't reach her eyes. "I didn't expect to see you for hours," she said.

He shrugged. "I am the boss. I make my own hours."

She looked at her baby and smiled, only this time it was genuine. He tried not to let that bother him. "It must be nice," she said, her voice a little higher and singsongy as she directed it at the baby.

"Indeed."

The baby gurgled in response, his little lips spreading in a grin. Drago watched as he picked up a fuzzy toy cat and put the ear in his mouth. Drago had been around babies before, in the commune his mother had once dragged them to on some tiny island somewhere he'd tried to forget, but he'd never really had anything to do with them. The older children had been expected to take care of the babies while their parents worked in the vegetable gardens—and got high in the evenings—but Drago's one major act of rebellion, before his mother had left the commune and tried to use him to get money from the Di Navarras again, had been to refuse to help with the babies.

Instead, he'd had to pick vegetables and hoe rows. He suppressed a shudder and folded himself into a nearby chair. Holly's brows rose. And then she turned toward her baby and started to gather him up.

"Why don't I take Nicky and get out of your way—"

"No. Stay." She stiffened, and he sighed. "Please stay. I need to talk to you."

She let the baby go and he threw the cat. Then he picked up a toy banana and started to chew on that.

"I'm all ears," she said brightly, though her eyes were wary.

"Do you have a copy of his birth certificate?"

The color drained from her face. "Why?"

Drago felt there was something he was missing here, but he wasn't quite sure what it could be. "For his passport. We have to take him to the passport office and apply in person, because he is a baby and it's his first."

She dropped her gaze. "All right," she said quietly.

"Is his father named on the certificate?"

Her head snapped up again. There was definitely fear in those pretty blue eyes. A wave of violence washed over him. He wanted, more than anything in that moment, to make her feel safe from the bastard who'd abandoned her and her child.

"If he is, then he must approve of you taking the baby from the country," he explained. "If not, it does not matter."

Holly seemed to wilt as she shook her head. "No, he's not named. He would have had to be there to sign it, and that wasn't going to happen."

Drago smiled to reassure her. "Good. Then you are safe. All will be well."

"Yes, I—I suppose so."

She turned to look at her baby, and his heart pinched. She loved the child so much. What would it have been like to have a mother who'd loved him that way? A mother who did everything for his benefit instead of for her own?

He would never know.

"There's nothing to worry about, Holly," he said. "Everything will be fine."

"Of course," she said. But she didn't sound reassured.

CHAPTER EIGHT

EVERYTHING WAS NOT going to be fine. Holly sat in the limo with Drago, Nicky tucked into his carrier, as they whisked their way through the streets of New York City on the way to the passport office. In her bag, she had Nicky's birth certificate and the forms she'd filled out for their passports.

She could still see the box that had made her heart drop to her toes: parents' names. She'd filled in only her side, because in Louisiana a father had to sign the birth certificate in order to be named. Drago wasn't on Nicky's birth certificate. No one was.

Still, it made her nervous. What if the passport office wanted more information? What if Drago were sitting beside her when they demanded it? How would she answer? How *could* she?

Holly pressed a hand to her stomach and concentrated on breathing in and out. There was still no sign of a contract, and they were on their way to get passports. It could all fall apart here. She could find herself on a plane home in just a few hours.

She would never see Drago again. That thought twisted her belly tighter than before. The scent of her fear was sharp, like cold steel against her tongue. She tried to ignore it, tried to focus on the other scents in the car. Warm leather, soft powdery baby, sensuous man. She closed her eyes and savored that last one as if it would soon be gone.

"What's the matter, Holly?"

She whipped around to look at Drago. His sharp gaze raked her. Belatedly, she smiled, trying to cover her distress. "Nothing at all."

One eyebrow rose in that superior manner of his. "I don't believe you."

She clasped her hands together in her lap. "Believe what you like, but I'm fine."

His frown didn't go away. "Would it help you to know that my lawyers have finished drafting your contract?"

Her heart did a slow thump against her chest. The contract. If only she had that already signed, she wouldn't worry as much. *Wrong.* Of course she would. Because she'd been lying to Drago from the moment he'd walked back into her life.

And, as she knew from bitter experience, he didn't handle deception very well.

"Oh? That's good."

His brows drew down. "You don't sound very enthused. Considering how insistent you've been, I find this rather odd."

Holly swallowed. "I'm very enthused," she said with false brightness. "What do you want from me? A happy dance right here in my seat?"

"Not precisely."

She rolled her eyes, tried to play it off. "I'm happy, Drago. Ecstatic."

He watched her a moment more. "Fine," he said, before dropping his gaze to his tablet once more.

Holly turned to look out the window at the traffic, her heart thrumming. She had to tell him the truth. Not right now, certainly, but soon. It was the right thing to do, no matter how much it terrified her. Once she had the contract, once it made sense to do so, she would have to find a way.

Provided it didn't all fall apart before she got that far.

The car pulled to a stop in front of a building on Hudson Street, and Drago opened the door. When they were standing on the sidewalk, Holly holding Nicky's carrier, she looked over at Drago, who was getting the diaper bag from the limo.

"You can come back and get us," she said. "I'll call when I'm done."

He looked imposing as he straightened to his full height and gazed down at her. He was dressed in a custom suit, navy blue, with a crisp white shirt and no tie. The pale blue diaper bag with the smiling monkey on it looked completely out of place against that elegant backdrop.

And yet he held it as though he could care less that the rich and entitled CEO of one of the most important cosmetics companies in the world might look just a little ridiculous. Or a little too appealing for a tabloid photo.

Holly cast her gaze up and down the street, but nobody with a camera emerged to snap a shot. Thank goodness.

"I'm going with you," Drago said.

"I don't see why," she returned. "I can handle it alone. Or you could send a lackey. Surely you have work to do."

"I have a cell phone and a tablet, Holly. I can work, I assure you."

She tried to swallow down her fear. It tasted like bitter acid. "I won't run away, Drago, if that's what you're worried about."

A preposterous suggestion that he'd be worried about her leaving, but it was the only thing she could think of.

"Holly, for goodness' sake, just turn around and walk into the building. We have an appointment and you're going to make us late."

She glared at him a moment more, her stomach dancing with butterflies—and then she heaved a sigh. "Fine, but don't blame me if it takes six hours and you're bored silly. I told you not to come."

Thankfully, it did not take six hours. But Holly's fear refused to abate while they waited. When they were finally shown into an office and it was time to hand over the paperwork, Holly snatched the diaper bag from Drago and fished out the papers with trembling hands. Then she handed them directly to the clerk.

The clerk was a typical bureaucrat, going over everything in triplicate. At one point, the woman looked up at Drago. He was flipping through files on his tablet and didn't seem to notice, but Holly's heart climbed into her throat as she waited for the woman to say something.

Then the clerk met Holly's gaze for a long moment. Finally, she seemed to give a mental shrug, and the moment was over. A short while later, they were on their way back to Drago's apartment, the passports safely tucked away in Holly's purse.

Holly felt a little shell-shocked over the whole thing. When they arrived at Drago's, she took Nicky and put him down for his nap. Then she climbed into bed and lay there, staring at the ceiling, her stomach still churning with guilt and fear. It wound its way through her belly, her bones, her heart, curling and squeezing until she thought she would choke on it.

She'd overcome another obstacle, gotten one step closer to the goal. Her luck was holding, but for how much longer?

She needed to tell Drago the truth before her luck ran out, but she was caught in an infinite loop of her own making. There was no scenario in which she could envision telling him and it not exploding in her face.

Once she signed the contract, she would tell him. Once she had the guarantee that she'd have money to take care of her baby, she could admit the truth. And then, even if he threw her out again when it was over, it would be fine. Everything would be fine.

But she couldn't quite make herself believe it.

When Holly finally emerged from her room a couple of hours later, it was because she was hungry and couldn't stay hidden any longer. She hoped that Drago would have gone out for the evening, so she didn't have to face him right now, but of course nothing ever went the way she hoped.

He looked up as she tiptoed into the kitchen. Her stomach slid down to the marble floor and stayed there.

"I was just looking for something to eat," she said casually.

"There's Chinese takeout," he said. "It's in the warming drawer."

She couldn't help but look at him in surprise. "You eat Chinese takeout?"

He shrugged. "Doesn't everyone?"

Not billionaires, she thought. She expected they ate lofty meals in the kinds of restaurants he'd taken her to the last time she was in New York. Or meals prepared at home by their personal chefs. Which he did happen to have.

"I figured that would be too, um, basic for you."

He laughed and a trickle of warmth stirred inside her. She loved that laugh more than she should. He was sitting at the expansive kitchen island with papers arrayed around him and an open laptop off to one side. Just a tycoon and his paperwork. Quite a different picture from the one she usually made at her worn Formica table every month, trying to make too little money stretch too far.

Chinese takeout had been a luxury. And Gabi was usually the one who'd bought it, against Holly's protests.

Save your money, Gabi. Don't waste it on me.

It's not a waste. Eat.

The memory of her and Gabi perched on the sofa in

front of the television, eating from containers, made her feel wistful. And lonely.

"Holly, I'm a man like any other," Drago said. "I like lobster and champagne, I like Kobe beef, I like truffles—but I also like Chinese takeout, hotdogs from a cart and gyros sliced fresh at a street fair."

She very much doubted he was like other men. But the idea of him eating a hot dog he'd bought from one of the carts lining the city streets fanned the warmth inside her into a glow.

"Next you'll be telling me you like funnel cakes and deep-fried candy bars."

"Funnel cakes, yes. Candy bars, no."

She pictured him tearing off bites of funnel cake, powdered sugar dusting his lips, and fresh butterflies swirled low in her belly. "Will wonders never cease?"

He grinned and then stood and walked over to the warming drawer. He wore faded jeans and a dark T-shirt, and his feet were bare. It was entirely too intimate and sexy, especially since the sky was dark and the city lights sparkled like diamonds tossed across the horizon.

She didn't know why that made it more intimate, but it did.

Drago pulled open the drawer and took out several containers of food. "There's a variety here. Mu shu pork, sweet-and-sour chicken, Mongolian beef, kung pao shrimp, black-pepper fish, lo mein, fried rice…"

Holly could only gape at him. "Gracious, was there a party tonight and I missed it?"

He shrugged, completely unselfconscious. "I didn't know what you liked, so I ordered several different things."

He set the containers on the counter, and Holly walked over to peer at the contents. Her stomach rumbled. It all looked—and smelled—wonderful. Drago set a plate and some wooden chopsticks on the counter.

"Thank you," she said softly. And then, though it embarrassed her, "But I'll need a fork."

He pulled open a drawer and took out a variety of silverware—forks and spoons so she could dip out the food—and set them down without a word about her inability to use chopsticks. It was a silly thing, but she was ridiculously grateful that he didn't tease her about it.

He walked back to his seat at the island, and Holly started to fill her plate. She thought about retreating to her room with the food, but he'd been so nice to order it all and she didn't want to be rude.

Holly turned and set the plate on the island. But instead of sitting, she stood and dug her fork into the kung pao shrimp. The flavors exploded on her tongue—spice and tang and freshness. Far better than anything she'd ever had from the lone Chinese restaurant in New Hope, where everything was either hidden under too much breading or soaked in sauce.

"I have your contract here," Drago said softly, and her belly clenched. "When you're done, we'll go over it."

She wanted to shove the food away and see it now, but she forced herself to keep chewing. She'd been unable to eat breakfast or lunch and now she was starving. If she didn't eat now, she didn't know if she would be able to. Her nerves swirled and popped like ice dropped on a hot grill. She was so close to having security for her baby. So close.

She put the fork down. "I have to see it now," she said. "I'll never be able to wait."

Drago frowned. "Only if you promise to keep eating," he said, picking up a sheaf of papers from the pile next to him.

"I will."

He came over and stood beside her, and her body was suddenly made of rubber. She wanted to lean into him, into his heat, and rest there while he explained what was in the papers. But she didn't. She forced herself to remain stiff, forced herself to keep forking food into her mouth while Drago pulled up the top sheet and laid it down.

"This is a basic contract," he said. "You'll appear in the ads, if all goes well with the test shots, for the next year. You'll be available for appearances to promote the perfume—industry functions, parties, etc.—and for more shoots as necessary. In exchange, you'll receive five hundred thousand dollars—"

Holly nearly choked on a bite of Mongolian beef. Drago glanced down at her, one brow lifted curiously.

"Sorry," she said a few moments later, after she'd gulped water from her glass and coughed enough to embarrass herself thoroughly.

"If the test shots aren't good," Drago continued while she mentally reeled over the sum he'd just named, "if we decide you aren't right after all, you'll receive a fifty-thousand-dollar severance fee and all your expenses for returning home."

Fifty thousand was still a lot of money. She could do something with fifty thousand. She could find a decent job, afford a better apartment. But half a million? Heavens above.

It was far more than she'd hoped—and yet a part of her was oddly disappointed. This wasn't how she'd envisioned her future. She wanted to work for a top company like Navarra Cosmetics. But she didn't want to stand in front of a camera and be the face of a fragrance. She wanted to *create* the fragrance.

But she had no choice. Since Nicky had come into her life, her desires took a backseat.

"What about my perfume?" she asked.

He flipped a couple of pages and tapped his finger on a line. "It's here. You get a half-hour appointment. Nothing more, and there are no guarantees."

"Do I get the appointment even if you decide not to keep me for the campaign?"

"Yes."

Her heart took up residence in her throat. "All right." She set down her fork and wiped her fingers on her napkin. "Can I read it?"

He pushed the contract toward her. "Take your time. But it needs to be signed tonight, *cara*. We leave for Italy tomorrow."

She'd thought her chest couldn't get any tighter, but she was wrong. "So soon?"

Drago looked so imposing standing there, hands in pockets, watching her. "*Sí*. There is no time to waste."

Holly perched on a bar stool and began to read the contract from beginning to end. There was a lot of legalese, but it was straightforward enough for her to understand. If the test shots went well, she got a lot of money. If they didn't, she still got money. And she got a chance to present her perfume to the head of Navarra Cosmetics, which was all she'd ever wanted in the first place.

When she finished reading, Drago laid a pen down in front of her. She glanced up at him, met his gaze. He seemed…very self-satisfied. The heated look on his face sent a sizzle of sensation straight to her core.

Her body softened, her insides melting as if she'd drunk a glass of wine. She felt fluid, languid. And intensely in need of his touch.

Holly picked up the pen, concentrated on the warm, smooth feel of the expensive barrel in her fingers. Anything that would take her attention from Drago. Anything that would make her heart stop tripping along as though it was running a marathon. Finally, she took a deep breath and pushed the pen across the signature line. Then she laid it on the table.

"*Grazie, cara,*" Drago said, reaching for the documents.

He shoved them into an envelope and then made a quick call to someone. A moment later, a man appeared in the doorway to the kitchen. Holly blinked as Drago handed him the envelope.

"You had someone waiting?" she asked when the man was gone.

"It is a courier, and yes, he was waiting to take these back to my attorney."

"But I was in my room," she said inanely.

"This I know," he replied. "But he only just arrived before you came out. I was coming to get you in five more minutes."

"Oh."

He was still looking at her, his gaze somehow both hot and assessing at the same time. "Feel better?" he asked.

Holly swallowed. Her mouth was dry. "Truthfully, I'm not sure. I'm not a model," she added, as if he didn't know.

His eyes sparkled with humor as he went back to his seat. "What is a model, except someone who advertises a product? You are not a professional, no. But you will learn."

"I don't want to be a model," she told him truthfully. "I want to make perfume."

She wondered if he was irritated with her for mentioning it, because he picked up his pen and tapped it on the island. "Ah, yes. And I have promised to let you present your fragrances to me. It seems to me as if you are gaining your chance in exchange for your participation."

Her heart thumped and her skin tingled with a different kind of excitement. "You won't be sorry," she said. "I know you won't."

She wasn't arrogant, but she knew her fragrances were good. And she wanted him to know it, too. She was confident in her ability, even if sometimes she felt like a total failure on the business side of things.

And a total failure elsewhere, as well. A cloud of doubt and fear drifted through her happiness, and she shivered. He was the father of her child and he did not know it. And she didn't know how to tell him. If not for that, everything would be perfect.

The thought made her want to giggle hysterically.

"What is wrong, Holly?" Drago asked, and she realized that something of her mood must show on her face.

"It's nothing," she told him carefully. "Nerves. Just a few days ago, I was taking drink orders. Now I'm here, in New York City again. With you. I keep waiting for the bottom to fall out."

He reached across the island and touched her hand. A shockingly strong current of heat flashed through her. Skin on skin. It was heavenly. Her entire body concentrated its attention on the limited surface area where they touched. It wasn't enough, and it was too much.

When he traced his thumb over her knuckles, she thought she would moan. She bit her lip to keep it from happening. *It's just skin*, she told herself. But it was his skin, his hand.

"You worry too much, *cara mia*," he said, his voice a sensual rumble deep in her core. "We're tied to each other now. For the foreseeable future."

He was talking about the contract and the Sky campaign. Though, for a single dangerous moment, she envisioned a different kind of bond. A bond between two people who wanted to be together. Two people who shared a child.

Holly licked her lips nervously. Her chest rose and fell as her breath came in short bursts. She wanted to run. She wanted to shove back from the island and flee before she fell any deeper into the morass. Before the truth came out and everything fell apart again.

Her life had been on the brink of disaster since Gran had died. She was accustomed to it. She was not accustomed to having hope. It terrified her. She tugged her hand away and tucked it into her lap.

Storm clouds fought a battle in Drago's expression. He looked frustrated and confused, and then he looked angry, his eyes hardening by degrees. Finally he sat back again. Incongruously, she wanted to reach out to him, beg him to touch her again.

"You have no reason to be scared of me," Drago said, shoving his chair back and standing. "I'm not a monster."

She tilted her head up to meet his hard gaze. But it stunned her to realize there was something more in his eyes. He looked…lost, alone. Her breath razored into her lungs.

"I don't think you're a monster," she said softly.

"I'm not sure I believe you."

Impulsively, she put her hand on his arm. His skin was warm beneath his sleeve, the muscle solid. His eyes were hooded as he stared at her, and a wave of fire sizzled through her body, obliterating everything in its path except this feeling between them.

This hot, achy feeling that made her body sing.

She dropped her hand away, suddenly uncertain. Why did she want to tempt fate again? Why did she want to take the risk and immolate herself in his flame?

Drago tilted her chin up when she would have looked away. "I don't understand you, Holly Craig. You are hot and cold, fierce and frightened. One minute I think you want…" He shook his head. "But then you don't. And I'll be damned if I can figure it out."

She tried to drop her chin, but he wouldn't let her. He forced her to meet his gaze. It was unflinching, penetrating. She trembled inside, as if he were reaching deep inside her soul and ferreting out all her secrets.

Except, he wasn't. He couldn't know what she kept hidden.

"It didn't end so well the last time," she told him. "Maybe that's what scares me."

He blew out a breath and closed his eyes for a long moment. "I make no apologies for what happened, Holly. You lied to me."

"I know. And I'm sorry for it. But I already told you why."

"Yes, you did." He sank onto the stool beside her and rubbed his palms along his jeans. "I don't like being lied to. And I don't like being used."

She wondered if he could see her pulse throbbing in her throat. Her palms were damp, but she didn't dare to wipe them dry while he watched her.

"I understand," she said.

"I don't think you do," he replied. He picked up a glass of some kind of liquor that had been sitting beside his paperwork and took a drink. She watched the slide of his throat, wondered how on earth such a thing could make her gut clench with desire.

"I've always been a Navarra, but I haven't always lived as one," he said quietly, after a long moment of silence.

Holly wrapped her arms around herself, her gut aching with the loneliness of his words.

"My parents were not married. My father was a playboy, a wastrel. My mother was easily corrupted, I think. When he wouldn't marry her, she might have had a bit of a breakdown." He shrugged, and she wondered what he did not say. "They were together for a couple of years, at least. I was a baby when he left her. He died in a car accident not too long after that. And that's when my mother started trying to use me to get things from his family. She spent years trotting me out in front of my uncle, demanding money and then spending it all foolishly."

"Babies need a lot of things," she said. "Maybe she didn't have enough, and…"

The fire in his eyes made her words die. She swallowed, her soul hurting so much for him. And for the woman who'd tried to raise him alone.

"She had enough, Holly. But not enough for her to get what she wanted."

"What did she want?"

His throat worked. "I wish to hell I knew." He threaded a hand through his hair, dropped it to his side again. "My uncle offered to take me in, but she refused to give me up."

Holly's stomach tightened. "I understand that. I wouldn't give Nicky up, either."

Drago leaned toward her. His expression was filled with pain and confusion. "She refused because she knew what she had. I was the golden goose, and periodically I brought her a golden egg. Eventually, my uncle offered her enough to let me go."

Holly's heart thudded painfully for him. But she understood why a mother wouldn't give up her child. Why she tried and tried to make it work before she finally gave in. What must Drago's mother have felt when she'd realized she couldn't keep him? That he would be better off with the Di Navarras than with her?

And why wouldn't Drago's uncle take them both? Why didn't he provide them with a home instead of an unthinkable option for a mother?

"I'm so sorry, Drago." What else could she say?

His features were bleak, ravaged. She wanted to put her arms around him and hold him tight. But she didn't. She didn't know if he would welcome it. If she could be strong enough to do it without confessing her own sins.

Oh, God, how could she ever tell him about Nicky now? He would *never* comprehend why she'd kept it a secret.

"I don't like to be used, Holly. I don't like the way it makes me feel."

"I understand," she said, her throat aching, her eyes stinging with tears. "And I'm sorry."

For so many things.

He sighed again. And then he shook his head as if realizing how much he'd said. "You should finish your dinner."

She looked at the food congealing on the plate. There was no way she could eat another bite. "I'm finished."

He stood again, shoved his hands into his pockets. He looked more lost than she would have ever thought possible.

"Do you see your mother much now?" she asked tentatively, imagining him as a little boy who must have felt so alone and confused when his mother had finally given in to his uncle's demands.

His eyes glittered as he turned to look at her. "I have not seen her since I was eleven and my uncle finally convinced her to sign over custody. And I never will again. She committed suicide six years ago."

Holly's heart hurt. "I'm sorry."

He shrugged with a lightness he could not possibly feel. "This is life."

"But…your mother," she said, her throat aching.

He reached out and slid his finger over her cheek, softly, lightly. "I believe you are a good mother, Holly Craig. But not all women are as dedicated as you."

His words pierced her in ways he would never know. What kind of mother kept a son from his father? What kind of mother struggled to raise him, to provide for him, when he could be the heir to all of this wealth? When he could have everything?

"Drago, I—" But she couldn't say it. Her throat closed up and nothing would come out.

He smiled, but it was not a real smile. It didn't reach his eyes. "Go to bed, Holly. Tomorrow will be a long day."

Like a coward, she fled.

CHAPTER NINE

HOLLY DIDN'T SLEEP very well. She kept waking up for myriad reasons. First, she couldn't stop thinking about Drago telling her, his eyes stark and lonely, that his mother had given him to his uncle and that he'd never seen her again. Then she kept worrying about Nicky, wondering if he was safe in his crib or if he was awake and crying and feeling alone.

She knew he wasn't crying, because she had a baby monitor. But every time she'd drift off to sleep, she'd hear him crying. Lost little boy. Lonely little boy. So she'd pop awake to silence—or as silent as the city could be with the cars rolling by far below, the honk of horns and squealing of brakes reaching high into the sky and finding her ears even in this protected environment.

She thought about Drago and Nicky and wondered how she would ever—or could ever—broach that topic. And she thought about getting on a plane and flying across a vast ocean to a place she'd never been. A place where she knew no one. Where she would be as lost as if she'd been plunked down on another planet.

Finally, Holly gave up and got out of bed. She showered and dressed in her best pair of jeans and a silky top with a cardigan she could put over it if she got chilled. She looked at herself in the mirror and felt woefully inadequate in her simple clothes.

Unsophisticated. Plain.

She leaned closer to the mirror, peering into it, trying to figure out what it was about her face that Drago wanted for his perfume. Freckles? She had a few of those, but she thought of them as imperfections rather than characteristics.

Her nose was small and straight, her cheekbones were on the plump side these days, and her mouth wasn't exactly a supermodel mouth. Her lips weren't luscious. They were average. Two pink lines that formed a pretty pout if she pursed her lips.

Her eyes were blue, but not spectacular. They weren't cornflowers or sapphires or any of those other things. They were just blue. Maybe sky-blue. Maybe just plain blue.

Holly brushed her hair into a ponytail and went to check on Nicky. He was awake, looking up at the mobile above him and kicking his little legs. Holly took him out of his crib and went into the kitchen to fix his bottle.

Drago looked up as she entered. He was sitting at the tall table facing the view, drinking coffee and reading the newspaper. Her heart flipped at the sight of him. She was getting a little tired of reacting so strongly to him, but she knew it wasn't going away. It had been there from the first moment, and would likely always be there.

"*Buongiorno, cara,*" he said.

"Good morning," she replied. Nicky pumped his arms and made a loud noise, and she laughed, unable to help herself. When she looked at Drago, he was smiling, though he looked tired. Perhaps he'd had trouble sleeping, too.

"He is rather, uh, energetic, yes?"

Holly nodded. "Oh, yes. He keeps me on my toes."

She rummaged in the refrigerator for the formula she'd mixed in the wee hours. Nicky hadn't drunk it all, so she'd put it away. Now she needed to heat it up. Which was hard to do with a squirming baby in her arms. She tried to shift him around, but he kept wiggling.

"Let me," Drago said, coming over and holding out his hands.

Holly's heart skipped several beats as she gazed up at him. Then she handed over his son. It felt as if someone had wrenched her child from her arms, so much did it hurt to give him to Drago at this very moment.

A ridiculous notion, but there it was. And then it was gone as Drago stood there with Nicky in his arms, looking suddenly uncertain. He held the baby out from his body with both hands, and Nicky kicked his legs back and forth.

"You won't break him," Holly said. "Cradle him to your chest and be sure to support his head."

Drago dragged his gaze from the baby to her. "That's it?"

Holly nodded. "That's it."

Drago did as she said, and she turned back to the counter, getting a bowl and filling it with water. She popped it into the microwave to heat and turned back to where Drago stood, looking down at Nicky warily.

She would have laughed if her heart hadn't been breaking.

"He's so small," Drago said.

"But getting bigger every day."

Nicky started to fuss and Drago shot her a panicked look.

"Bounce up and down a little bit," she said. Drago looked doubtful, but then he started to do as she said, and Nicky quieted. Holly bit her lip to keep from smiling at the sight of strong, handsome Drago di Navarra—playboy, billionaire cosmetics king—bouncing awkwardly with a baby in his arms.

But then her smile faded when she considered that Nicky was *his* baby and she still needed to tell him so.

After last night, after she'd understood how lonely his life had been, it felt terribly wrong not to tell him he had a son.

But the moment had to be right. And it wasn't now.

She turned to the microwave and took the water out, setting the bottle inside and then reaching for her baby. Drago seemed relieved as he turned him over. Holly bounced Nicky and said nonsensical things to him while Drago went back to his coffee and paper. But rather than pick up the paper, he watched her. She met his gaze, saw the confusion and heat in his beautiful gray eyes.

"You make me want the strangest things, Holly Craig," he said softly, and a hot feeling bloomed in her belly, her core.

"It's probably just indigestion," she said flippantly, and he laughed. But her heart thrummed and her blood beat and a fine sheen of sweat broke out on her upper lip and between her breasts.

What she really wanted to know was what kind of things. That was the question she wanted to ask, but was too scared to. *Coward.*

Yes, she was a coward, at least where Drago was concerned. Because there was something about him, something she desperately desired. And if she angered him, if he sent her away, then she wouldn't get that thing, would she? It wasn't just sex, though it was that, too.

It was…*something.*

He folded the paper and sat back to sip his coffee with one arm folded over his body. He wore faded jeans and a dark button-down shirt, and his muscles bulged and flexed as he moved his arm. Her knees felt weak.

"Yes, perhaps you are right," he said. "Perhaps I just haven't had enough coffee yet." He glanced at his watch and frowned. "We need to leave for the airport in an hour. Will you be ready?"

Her stomach spun. "Yes."

"Good." He stood then. "I have some paperwork to attend to first. I'll let you know when it's time."

He left her in the kitchen alone, and she fed Nicky while looking out over the early-morning mist wreathing Central Park. She grabbed a cup of coffee and a bagel from the bag of fresh ones sitting on the counter.

Soon, they were in the car and on their way to JFK airport. Traffic was insane in New York and they spent a lot of time sitting still. Drago worked on his laptop, and Holly gazed out the window while Nicky slept.

She must have dozed, because suddenly Drago was shaking her awake and she was clawing back the fog in her brain while trying to process what he was saying.

"Passports," she finally heard him say. "I need your passports."

She fished in her bag and dug them out. Drago took them from her and then she leaned back and closed her eyes again. It was several minutes before the uneasy feeling in her belly finally grabbed her brain and shook hard enough to drag her into alertness.

But it was already too late. She sat up ramrod straight to find Drago looking at her, his gaze as hard as diamonds, his face some combination of both disgust and rage.

She'd had every chance in the world, and she'd blown it. Drago wasn't stupid. He would have realized by now she hadn't told him the truth. And he would never believe she hadn't meant to deceive him.

He held a blue passport in his hand, opened to the first page. He turned it toward her. She didn't need to look at it to know what it said.

"Tell me, Holly, precisely how old your child is again. And then I want you to tell me once more about this married man you had an affair with."

* * *

Drago felt as if someone had put a vise around his neck and started twisting. He couldn't breathe properly and he had to concentrate very, very hard on dragging each breath in and then letting it out again. It was the only thing keeping him from raging at her and demanding a definitive answer right this instant.

He held the passport in a cold grip and watched the play of emotions across her face. Her eyes were wide, the whites showing big and bright, and her skin was flushed. Her mouth was open, but there was no sound coming out.

Then she went deadly pale as all that heat drained away. He kept waiting for her to explain. To tell him why her baby was three months old and not two. Not that it meant anything that the child was three months old. It didn't make the boy his. He kept telling himself that.

Drago hadn't noticed the baby's real age at first. Hadn't realized the implications. She'd been soft and sleepy and he hadn't wanted to wake her, but he'd needed the passports for when they went through the checkpoint to reach the private jets. She'd handed them to him and gone back to her nap, and he'd flipped them open, studying the details as the car crawled closer to the guard stand. He was a detail-oriented man.

Holly was twenty-four, which he already knew, and she'd been born in Baton Rouge. Nicholas Adrian Craig had been born in New Orleans a little over three months ago.

That detail had meant nothing to him at first. Nothing until he started to think about how long ago it had been that he'd first met Holly when she'd come to New York. It was a year ago, he remembered that, because he remembered quite well when he'd had to scrap all the photos from the false shoot and start over. The numbers were imprinted on his brain.

Even then, he'd had a moment's pause while he'd pictured pretty, virginal Holly rushing home to Louisiana and falling into bed with another man. He didn't like the way that thought had made him feel.

But then, as he'd pondered it, as he'd watched her sleep and let his gaze slide over to the sleeping baby in his car seat—the baby with a head of black hair and impossibly long eyelashes—another thought had taken hold.

And when it did, Drago felt as if someone had punched him in the gut. He'd struggled to breathe for the longest moment.

There was no way. No way this child could be his. Black hair and long lashes meant nothing. He'd used protection. He always used protection.

But there'd been that one time when the condom had torn as he was removing it, and he started to wonder if it had perhaps torn earlier.

And as that thought spiraled and twisted in his brain, doubt ignited in his soul. If it were true, how could she do such a thing? How could anyone do such a thing?

But he did not know that she had, he reminded himself. He did not know.

"Whose child is he, Holly?" Drago demanded, his voice as icy cold and detached as he could make it. Because, if he did not, it would boil over with rage and hurt.

She'd lied to him. And she'd used him, used the opportunity to get what she wanted from him. He thought of the contract she'd insisted on, the money he'd agreed to pay her, and his blood ran cold.

Her gaze dropped and a sob broke from her. She crammed her fist against her mouth and breathed deeply, quickly. And then, far quicker than he'd have thought possible, she faced him. Her cheeks and nose were red, and her eyes were rimmed with moisture.

"I tried to tell you," she said, and his world cracked

open as she admitted the truth. Pain rushed in, filling all the dark and lonely corners of his soul. The walls he'd put up, the giant barriers to hurt and feeling—they tumbled down like bricks made of glass. They shattered at his feet, sliced deep into his soul.

"What does that mean?" he snapped, still hoping she would tell him it was a mistake, that this child was not his and she hadn't kept that fact hidden from him for the past three months. For nine long months before that.

But he already knew she wouldn't. He knew the answer as certainly as he knew his own name. This child was a Di Navarra, and Drago had done exactly as his father had done—he'd fathered a child and abandoned it to a mother who thought nothing of living in squalor and leaving her baby with strangers.

He wanted to reach out and shake her, but he forced himself to remain still.

"It means," she said, her voice soft and thready, "that I wrote you a letter. That I called. That you turned me away and refused all contact."

He was still reeling from her admission.

"And I will wager you didn't try hard enough," he growled. "I never got a letter."

It staggered him to think she'd spent all those months carrying his child, and he hadn't even known it. He hadn't specifically refused contact with her, but he had a long-standing policy of not accepting phone calls from people—especially women—not on his approved list of business associates. As for the letter, who knew if she'd even sent one?

"Well, I sent it. It's not my fault if you didn't get it."

His vision was black with rage. "How convenient for you," he ground out. "You say you sent a letter, but what proof do I have? You could be lying. And you could have done more, if you'd really wanted to."

"Why would I lie about this? I was alone! I needed help! And not only that, but what else would you have had me do?" she snapped tearfully. "Fly to New York with my non-existent credit cards and prostrate myself across the floor in front of your office? I tried to get in touch with you, but it was like trying to call the president of the United States. They don't just let anyone in—and no one was letting me in to you!"

The moment she finished, her voice rising until it crackled with anger, the baby started to cry. Drago looked at the child—Nicky, Nicholas Adrian—and felt a rush of confusion like he hadn't known since he was a boy, when his mother would come into his bedroom and tell him they were leaving whatever place he'd finally gotten settled into.

He didn't like that feeling. If they were still in the apartment, he would have stalked out and gone for a run in the park. Anything to put some distance between him and this lying, treacherous woman. But he was stuck in this car and his head was beginning to pound.

Holly bent over and started trying to soothe the baby, ignoring him as she did so. She talked in a high voice, offered the child a pacifier and made shushing noises. A tear slipped down her cheek, and then another, and her voice grew more frantic.

"Holly."

She looked up at him, her eyes so full of misery. He felt a rush of something akin to sympathy, but he shoved it down deep. Locked it in chains. How could he feel sympathy for her when she'd lied to him? When she'd used him?

He hated her. And he would *not* let her get away with keeping his child from him. Not any longer.

"Calm down," he ordered tightly. "He senses your distress."

"I know that," she snapped. She turned back to the baby—his son—and began to unbuckle the straps holding him in the seat. Then she pulled him out and cradled him against her, rocking and shushing until his tears lessened. Finally, he took a pacifier and Holly seemed to wilt in relief.

"You've been in my house for nearly a week now," Drago said, his voice so icy it made him cold. "And you've kept the truth from me. You had every chance to tell me, Holly. Every chance. Just like before."

She didn't look at him, and he wanted to shake her until she did. The violence whipping through his body frightened him, though he knew he would never give in to it.

But he'd never been this shocked, this betrayed, before. His mother had sold him in the end, sold him for money and freedom to do as she liked, and even the pain of that didn't quite compare to this.

He had a child, a baby, and the only reason he knew it was because he could do math. If he hadn't figured it out, would she have ever told him? Or would she have done the job, taken the money and disappeared with his child?

Until she'd spent it all and needed more....

Drago shook himself. "You have nothing to say to me?" he demanded. "You would sit there after what you've done and refuse to explain yourself?"

Her head came up then. Her eyes were red-rimmed. "I didn't know how to tell you. I thought you might throw me out again."

He reeled. She was unbelievable. A user. A schemer. First it was perfume; now it was a child.

He despised her.

"I might still," he growled. He wouldn't be as tender as his uncle had been. He knew what could happen when you let a woman keep a child she couldn't take care of properly, and he would never allow that to happen to his own son. He would use the might and money at his disposal to make sure she never saw this boy again.

Her eyes widened with fear. God help him, he relished it. He wanted her to wonder, wanted her to suffer as he was suffering.

"You would do that to your own son?" she asked, her voice wavering.

The violence in his soul whipped to a frenzy. "Not to him, Holly. To *you*."

Fear was an icy finger sliding down her spine. It sank into her body, wrapped around her heart and squeezed the breath from her. Drago sat beside her, his handsome face far colder than she'd ever seen it before.

He hated her. She could see it clearly, and her heart hurt with the knowledge that any sort of closeness they might have been building was lost. Crushed beneath the weight of this new reality.

She was frozen in place, frightened with the knowledge that he could kick her out of his life and keep her son. That he would even try.

And then, like the sun's rays sliding from behind the clouds to melt an ice-encrusted landscape, the first fingers of flame licked to life inside her belly. They were weak at first, vulnerable to being crushed out of existence.

But Nicky stretched and reached up to curl his fingers into the edge of her cardigan, and a wave of pure love flooded her with strength.

She met Drago's cold stare with a determined look of her own. Her heart was a fragile thing in her chest, but she didn't intend to let him know it. "You will not separate me from my son. Not ever."

"You forget who has the power here, *cara*," he said tightly.

"And you forget who Nicky's legal parent is," she threw back at him.

His jaw was a block of granite. "There are ways of remedying that," he said, and her stomach dropped through the floor.

"No," she choked out. "No. There's nothing you can do to change it."

She would fight him with every ounce of strength she had left in her body to prevent it. He would never take Nicky away. Never.

He was not the same man she'd spent the past few days with. This man was infinitely darker, more frightening. "Everyone has a price, Holly. Even you."

She hugged her baby's little body to her. "You're wrong, Drago. I'm sorry if you had a bad childhood, and I'm sorry you think your mother traded you for money. But I love my son and I'm not giving him up. You don't have enough money to even make me think about it, much less ever do it."

His eyes glittered and she shivered. "We'll see about that, *cara.*"

He didn't say another word to her for the rest of the car trip. Instead, he got on the phone and started talking in rapid Italian. He made two or three calls before they reached the jet parked on the tarmac, and Holly's nerves were scraped raw by that time.

She wondered who he was talking to, what he was saying and what he planned to do. Was he talking to his lawyers? To someone who would bar her from the plane while he took Nicky and jetted off for Europe?

She held her baby tighter. She would never let him take this child from her. She wouldn't let anyone bar her from the plane and she would never accept money in exchange for Nicky.

There simply wasn't enough money in the world to make it worth her while.

When they reached the jet, Drago told her to hand Nicky over to Sylvia, who stood at the bottom of the stairs, smiling warmly. Holly cradled her baby close and refused, her heart hammering in spite of Sylvia's friendly greeting.

"You could fall on the steps," he said sharply, and her stomach banged with fear.

"I won't fall," she said. And then she started up the steps, one arm around her son, the other holding the metal railing until she was at the top and walking onto the plane. Drago was right behind her, so close she could smell his scent over the lingering aroma of jet fuel and the new smell of the plane's interior.

She could also smell the sharp scent of his anger, steely and cold. His body, however, was hot at her back, and she stepped away quickly, emerging into a spacious cabin.

The plane was much larger than the jet they'd flown on just a few days ago. This one was also incredibly luxurious. The interior gleamed with white leather, dark shiny wood finishes and chrome. There was a bar at one end, a couch with a television, and several other plush chairs.

"There are two bedrooms," Drago informed her. "And several bathrooms."

In the end, it turned out that one of the bathrooms was bigger than her entire bedroom had been in New Orleans. She knew Drago was wealthy—he was the head of a multinational corporation and heir to a cosmetics fortune—but she'd never quite realized the impact of all that money until this very moment, when she feared it was about to be arrayed against her. Yes, she'd signed a contract for half a million dollars, but she now realized how very tiny a drop in the ocean of wealth that was to a man like Drago di Navarra.

And it worried her. What if he did try to take Nicky away? She flinched as the door to the Jetway closed with a solid thump. Panic bloomed. She wanted off this plane. She wanted to take her baby—who she'd finally handed over to Sylvia now that they were firmly inside—and run down the stairs and into the terminal. Away from Drago. Away from the vessel that was about to take her across an ocean and put her somewhere she knew no one.

And had no power. Holly swallowed hard. She turned to go after Sylvia, to find her baby and at least be with him for the duration of the trip, since escape was now impossible.

But Drago was there, tall and commanding and so very distant as he gazed down at her, his handsome features set with disdain. An aching sadness unfolded itself within her as she thought back to last night and the Chinese food. She'd almost felt close to him then.

Almost.

"You will need to sit and buckle up," Drago said. "We'll be off the ground in a few minutes."

"I want to be with Nicky."

"Sylvia is taking care of him. That is what she is paid to do."

Holly tossed her ponytail over her shoulder. She could not let him see that he intimidated her, no matter how much he did. "My idea of how to raise a child isn't paying people to take care of him. Nicky needs me."

His eyes narrowed and she had a sudden, visceral feeling that she'd crossed a line somewhere.

"He will have only the best from now on, Holly. Sylvia is the best."

"And I am his mother," she said, her heart stinging with pain. She'd given Nicky everything she had, but of course it wasn't the best money could buy. She tilted her chin up. She had to be brave, assertive. "There's more to taking care of a child than money. He needs love and attention, and I give him that."

"Ah, yes," he said. "Such as when you dropped him with your neighbor and went to work in a casino. I'm sure he had plenty of love and attention then."

She felt as if he'd hit her. "I did the best I could," she

told him. "It wasn't as if you were there to help. And you weren't going to *be* there because I couldn't get in touch with you. You made it very clear that I was never to do so."

He shot up out of his seat and she took a step back instinctively. "To sell me perfume," he thundered. "You were never to contact me about your damn perfume!"

Her breath razored in and out of her lungs. "And how was I supposed to make sure you knew the difference if you'd already ordered your secretary to deny my calls?" she yelled back. "Was I supposed to send you mental signals and hope that did the trick?" She picked up a pretend phone and held it to her ear. "Oh, look," she mimicked, "it's Holly Craig calling. But this time it's *important*!"

His teeth ground together and anger clouded his features. Out of the corner of her eye, she saw a flight attendant moving carefully around them. That was when she realized they were making a spectacle.

She turned and flung herself down in a plush club chair and buckled her seat belt. Her cheeks sizzled with heat and her nerves snapped with tension. Her fingers trembled as she gripped the arms of the seat.

Drago dropped into a chair beside her, though there were plenty of other empty seats, and buckled himself in. Anger rolled off his body like fallout from a nuclear explosion.

"If you had wanted to tell me," he snarled, "you would have found a way. Instead, you let me believe this baby belonged to another man. A married man who abandoned you and left you to starve in the cold. You lied to me, Holly. And you would have kept on lying if I hadn't figured it out."

"I didn't say it was a married man. You *assumed*—"

"And you agreed!" he shot back. "What else was I to think, the way you acted?" His voice sliced into her. "You were worried about getting caught in your lies."

She whipped around to face him. "Yes, I was worried, Drago! I was worried because you promised me a way out of my situation. And if you learned the truth, and reacted the way you had the last time, I'd be back at square one. Only, this time I had my son to think about. And no way in hell was I letting you hurt *him*."

His eyes narrowed dangerously. She realized then, looking at him, that the roiling surface of his anger went far, far deeper than she'd ever thought. He was civilized— but barely.

"Did you ever consider for one moment, for one damn moment, that I might have a wholly different reaction to the knowledge I'd fathered a child? Especially when I told you about my own circumstances as a boy?"

She swallowed. "Not at first," she said. She'd endured the humiliation of being thrown out of his life before, when she'd done nothing wrong, and she couldn't take that chance with her child. "But I was going to tell you. I wanted the time to be right."

He leaned in toward her, his gray eyes hard and angry. "And why should I believe a word you say?"

Her eyes felt gritty. "No reason," she whispered.

"Precisely." He leaned back again, his body stiff with anger as the jet began to move. "You are going to regret your silence, Holly Craig," he told her. "You are going to regret it very much when I am through with you. This I promise."

CHAPTER TEN

THEY LANDED IN Italy late that night. It was dark and Holly couldn't see anything. She had no idea where they were, though she thought she'd read that the Di Navarras were from Tuscany. She didn't get a chance to ask Drago, because he got into a different car than she did. She was with Sylvia and Nicky, which was a great relief after the tension-filled flight over the Atlantic.

As soon as they'd been airborne, Drago had disappeared. He'd ripped open the seat belt and shot up from his chair like a hunted creature. Then he'd stalked toward the rear of the plane and hadn't returned. When she'd inquired of a flight attendant, she'd learned that Drago had an office. She didn't see him again until right before they landed.

He'd still glared at her with the same fury as he had hours before. His anger had not abated in the least, and that chilled her.

The cars wound their way through the night until they reached a grand estate that seemed to sit on a hill of its own. There were tall pencil pines and arbors of bougainvillea they passed on their way up the drive.

Holly wasn't even certain she'd been taken to the same place as Drago until she got out of the car and saw him gesturing to a man, who eventually bowed and then turned to give quick orders to the line of men and women standing behind him. Suitcases were hefted into many hands, and then they disappeared behind the tall double wooden doors of the villa.

Drago didn't spare her so much as a glance as he entered the house. Holly's heart pinched. And then she sniffed. She told herself that she did *not* miss the way he'd looked at her this morning when he'd told her she made him want things he'd never wanted before. It had been an illusion, nothing more. The sooner she forgot about it—the sooner she armed herself for this new reality—the better.

She was shown to a large corner room filled with antiques, Oriental carpets, gilded mirrors and overstuffed couches and chairs. There was a television in a cabinet, and a huge four-poster bed against one wall.

"I will need a crib," she said to the woman who was explaining how the television worked.

The woman blinked. "There is no need, Signorina Craig," she began in her perfect English. "The child is to stay in the nursery."

For the first time, Holly realized Sylvia was not right behind her, carrying Nicky. She'd been so tired, so lost in her own thoughts, that she hadn't noticed they were no longer with her. Holly's blood beat in her ears as fresh panic shot through her. "The nursery? And where is that?"

The woman, a pretty woman with dark hair coiled on her head, continued to smile. As if she'd been told to always be polite to the guests, no matter how frantic they sounded.

"It is not far," she said.

Ice formed in Holly's veins. "Not far? I'm afraid that's unacceptable."

The woman inclined her head in that slight manner that reeked of studied politeness. "Signore Di Navarra has ordered it, Signorina Craig. I cannot contravene *il padrone's* orders."

Holly didn't even bother to argue. She simply turned on her heel and strode from the room. There was a shocked silence behind her, and then the woman called her name, rushing after her. Holly picked up her pace, roving blindly through the corridors, taking turns that led into dead ends and empty rooms, doubling back on herself and trying again.

She didn't realize she was crying until she stopped in a hallway she'd already been in once before, looking right and left, and heard a sound like a sob. It took her a minute to realize the sound had come from her.

She squeezed her eyes shut, gritted her teeth. She would *not* lose control. She would not. She would find Nicky— or she would find Drago and give him a piece of her mind he wasn't likely to ever forget.

Holly came upon a set of stairs and dashed down them until she found herself in the huge circular entry. The foyer was quiet now, compared to just a few minutes ago, but she stood in the cavernous space until she heard a sound. A footstep, the clink of a glass, something. She moved toward it until it she heard a voice.

And then she burst into a room ringed with tall shelves that were lined with books. It took her a moment to realize the damn man had a library. A light burned softly on a desk, and a man stood behind it, his back to her, talking on a phone.

Drago.

Rage and longing filled her, rushing through her body in twin waves. She didn't understand how she could be so angry and so needy at the same time. How she could want to rage at him and hold him at once. She took a step forward, and Drago turned at the sound, his silvery eyes gleaming with anger when he saw her. He finished the call and set his phone on the desk.

"What do you want, Holly?"

She took another halting step forward, her lungs burning, her chest aching. "How dare you?" she spat. "How *dare* you!"

Drago looked bored. "How dare I what, *cara mia*? You must say what you mean. Or get out until you can."

"Nicky. You've put him in the nursery. Away from me." She could hardly get the words out she was so angry.

A muscle leaped in his jaw. "He is a baby. The nursery is where he belongs."

"He is my son, and I want him with me," she growled.

"He is my son, too, and I want him in the nursery. He is safe there."

Violence rocked through her. "Are you trying to say he's not safe with me?"

"And if I am?"

She couldn't answer that. Not without committing violence. "Why do you even have a nursery? You aren't married, you don't have children—"

The look on his face could have melted steel. "I do now, don't I?"

Holly swallowed. "You know what I mean."

"I do indeed."

She ignored the taunt in his voice. He was doing this deliberately. Trying to prove his mastery over her. His power. He wanted her scared. "How can you have a nursery?"

He came around the desk, too cool for words, and leaned against it. Then he folded his arms over his chest, and the fabric of his dark shirt bulged with muscles. Where had he gotten a physique like that? Clearly, he worked out— but she had no idea when he had the time, since he always seemed to be running his business.

Holly shook her head to clear it. She did *not* need to worry about Drago's muscles. They weren't hers to explore. Nor did she care.

"This estate has been in my family for generations,

cara. There has always been a nursery. It's been in disuse for quite some time, but a phone call fixed that. Did you think my son would have nowhere to stay once we arrived? Did you believe I would not even think to see to his comfort and care? Such a low—and dangerous, I might add—opinion you have of me."

There was menace in his voice. And heat. Oddly, it was the heat that interested her. She studied his face, the hard planes and angles of his perfectly sculpted features, and her pulse thrummed.

She needed to focus, and not just on this man before her. "I want my baby with me. He's not used to being alone."

"He is not alone, Holly. He has a nanny."

"He doesn't need a nanny," she blurted. "He only needs me."

Drago straightened to his full height. She wanted to take a step back, but she held her ground. "He needs more than a mother who struggles to make ends meet." His voice was like a whip. "More than a mother who leaves him with strangers while she works twelve to sixteen hours a day."

Pain exploded in her chest. She sucked in a deep breath and willed herself not to cry. Of course he would hit her where it hurt the most. Of course. "I gave him the best I could, Drago. I will always give him the best I can."

"Yet I can give him more. Better. How can you wish to deny him that?"

"I never said I did. But you will not separate us. Not ever."

His eyes narrowed. "Such conviction. And yet I wonder where this conviction stems from. Have you found your own golden goose, Holly? Will you cling to this child until you've bled as much money from his existence as you can?"

Holly didn't even think before reacting. The distance between them shrank too quickly for her to be aware of what she was doing. The next thing she knew, she was standing right in front of him and Drago was holding her wrist in an iron grip. Her open hand was scant inches from his face.

She jerked in his grasp, but he didn't let her go. Instead, he yanked her closer, until their bodies were pressed together, breast to belly to hip. It was the first time they'd been this close in a year, and the shock ricocheted through her.

Her palms came up to press against his chest—that hard, masculine chest that had filled her dreams for months. Holly forced herself to concentrate on her anger, not on the way it felt to be this close to Drago again—as if she'd come home after years away. As if she'd found water in the desert after going without for so long.

It was an illusion.

"You're a cruel bastard," she spat. "I love my son more than my own life. There is nothing I wouldn't do for him. *Nothing!*"

"Prove it."

She blinked up into his cold, handsome face. "What do you mean?"

"Walk away, Holly. Give him to me, and I will make sure he has the best money can buy for the rest of his life."

A shudder racked her. And then the heat of anger filled her. How dare he try to manipulate her emotions this way?

"I won't," she said. "No matter what you do to me, I won't."

His eyes glittered. One dark eyebrow lifted. "Are you certain?"

Her heart thumped. "Very."

Drago pushed her away and walked back around the desk. Then he sat down and opened a drawer, ignoring her for the moment. Her nerves stretched tight.

Finally he looked up, his handsome face cold and blank.

"There is a party tomorrow night for some industry people. You will attend."

Holly folded her arms across her chest, hugging herself as the wind dropped from her sails. "A party?"

His gaze was sharp, hard. "Yes. You signed a contract. You are the new face of Sky. You will be by my side tomorrow night."

Her throat ached. She couldn't very well refuse, and they both knew it. "Where is my son?"

Drago's look changed to one of supreme boredom. "The nursery is down the hall from your room. To the right. I imagine you went left when you departed, yes?"

She felt like a fool. How did he do that to her? "Yes."

His gaze dropped to his papers. "We are done. Good night."

When she was gone, Drago dropped his head into his hands and sat there at his desk, being very quiet and very still. Quite simply, she turned him upside down. This morning, his world had been right. He'd enjoyed having Holly in his home, oddly enough. He'd looked forward to talking to her. To watching her mother her baby.

His baby.

Drago swallowed. It felt like razor blades going down his throat. His entire day on the plane had been spent working in his office, making calls, viewing reports, talking until his voice gave out. He'd tried to distract himself, but all the while his chest had been tight and his eyes had stung and he'd wanted to go back into the main cabin and wrap his hands around Holly Craig's pretty neck.

And then he'd wanted to strip her naked and take her up against the wall. Bend her over a table. Lay her spread-eagled on the floor.

He hadn't cared how he would have her. He'd just wanted her.

And it angered him. How could he want a woman like her? A woman who'd lied to him, who'd kept his child hidden from him for the sake of a damn contract? She'd had every chance to tell him the truth, starting from the first moment when he'd walked into that hovel of an apartment and ending with the moment he'd discovered the truth for himself.

She hadn't done so, and he didn't believe she'd had any intention to—or at least not until it most benefited her. When she needed more money, when she'd spent everything she had, just like his mother had always done, she'd come with her hand out.

But even if she'd wanted to tell him, even if he gave her the benefit of the doubt, how could he forgive her for the lie for the past year? She said she'd written to him—who the hell wrote letters these days?—and tried to call.

He wasn't easy to get in touch with—but it wasn't impossible. Just last month, a woman he'd met at a party had managed to get a call through to his home number. He was not impossible to find. And Holly Craig had been to his home, unlike most of the women he went out with.

What if he'd never gone to New Orleans? When would she have come to him?

Drago shuddered. His mother hadn't taken him to his uncle for money until he'd been nearly four years old. He could still remember the look on Paolo's face when they'd shown up here at the villa. Shock, anger and confusion. And then Uncle Paolo and his mother had gone into his uncle's office while he was supposed to have played outside.

Instead, he'd stood in the foyer and listened to the raised voices. He'd been too young to know what they were fighting about, but he remembered the tension—and he remembered being scared and feeling as if it was his fault.

He would *never* allow his son to feel that way. As if he

was the source of everyone's problems. As though he was a commodity to be bartered again and again.

Drago shoved back from the desk and stood. One way or the other, he was taking control of his child's life immediately. Holly Craig had stood in his way long enough. No more.

He would own her completely—or he would send her away for good.

Holly was nervous. She stood just inside the house, listening to the sounds of laughter and music and chatter on the terrace outside, and felt as if her heart would pound from her chest. Drago had informed her only this morning that the party was taking place here, at his villa—and all her plans to beg out of the event with a headache or a stomachache or something else had come crashing down around her head.

She'd had no idea how she was supposed to attend a party when all she had were jeans and tennis shoes, but a tall, elegant woman—accompanied by three assistants—had arrived immediately after Drago's announcement with a selection of gowns and shoes and jewelry. Within two hours, Holly had a gown for the event and all the accessories to match—even down to the fine, lacy underwear.

She'd wanted to wear her own undergarments, but the woman—Giovanna—had looked at her in horror when she'd suggested it. When everything arrived that afternoon, Holly had still intended to wear her own things—until she'd taken a good look at the dress and realized the underwear was designed to go with it, and that her own would not be flattering to the cut of the gown at all. Vanity won out over stubbornness, and now she stood there in the shadows in a strapless flowing white gown, sewn with iridescent cream sequins, and felt so very out of her element that it frightened her.

She'd never worn anything so beautiful or expensive in her life. Her senses, already highly tuned, were sharpened tonight. Every scent bombarded her with sensation until she was afraid she'd have a pounding headache before the night was through. After she'd dressed, she'd taken one sniff of the bottle of Sky that Drago had sent up for her and knew she couldn't wear it.

There was nothing wrong with the fragrance, but it wasn't her. Instead, she spritzed on Colette and, head high and heart pounding, left her room and made the descent to the first level. She'd thought Drago would be waiting for her, but there was no one. The party was outside, in the glowing Tuscan evening. The sun was behind the horizon, but the sky was still golden and the landscape below undulated in darkening shadows of green and black.

Holly felt like a spy watching through the windows. And she felt as if she didn't belong. She wanted to go back upstairs to the nursery and curl up on the couch there with Nicky. Holly lifted her head. She was doing this for Nicky. For his future.

"I don't especially like crowds, either," a voice said, and Holly spun around to find a man standing behind her. He hadn't been in the room when she'd walked in. He was tall, handsome—not so handsome as Drago—and he was smiling at her. He held out his hand as he walked up. "I don't believe we've met. I am Santo Lazzari."

Holly held out her hand as butterflies swirled in her belly. Santo Lazzari of House of Lazzari was powerful in his own right. House of Lazzari wasn't a cosmetics firm, though they did sell a selection of designer perfumes in their stores to go along with their clothing and handbags. "Holly Craig. But how did you know…"

"That you weren't Italian?" He laughed. "My dear, Drago has spoken of nothing else since this party began."

His eyes narrowed as he studied her. "You are the new face of Sky."

Holly dropped her gaze as a blush spread over her cheeks. She was going to have to get used to this, even if she felt like an imposter. Even if she felt as if Santo Lazzari was mocking her, picking her apart and finding her lacking.

"I did tell Drago I'm not a model, but he seems to believe I'm what he wants." Her skin heated further as she realized what she'd said. "For the campaign," she added hastily.

Santo laughed. "Yes, Drago is like that." He took a step closer, sniffing the air around her. "Is this the perfume? It smells different from how I remembered."

"Um, well, no," she stammered. "I mean, yes, it's perfume. But it's not Sky."

Santo's gaze sharpened. "A new fragrance? Drago has not mentioned this before."

Beads of moisture rose on Holly's skin. Should she tell this man what she was wearing? Or should she change the subject? But how could she let a chance like this go by, especially when Drago was threatening to take her baby away? Telling Santo Lazzari about Colette could be insurance against the future. Drago was certain not to buy her perfume now, no matter that she had an ironclad appointment to pitch it to him.

"It's my own blend."

Santo's eyebrows lifted. "Is it, now?" His eyes gleamed with sudden interest. He held out his arm to her. "Come, Holly Craig, tell me more about this scent as we enter the party. I want to hear all about it."

Holly hesitated a moment longer. What would Drago think if she entered the party on another man's arm? But then the truth hit her, and it made her ache.

Drago would not care in the least. He despised her now.

No doubt he would think she was searching for another rich victim.

She told herself she did not care what he thought. She told herself it didn't matter, that the tentative closeness she'd thought they were building had been only an illusion. Drago did not care about her. He cared only about punishing her.

Holly smiled and put her arm through Santo's.

Drago stood with some of his best clients, telling them about his plans for Sky, when a collective hush fell over the gathering. Male eyes gleamed with appreciation as they gazed at a point beyond his shoulder. Drago turned to see what new arrival had caught their attention so thoroughly—

And gaped in stunned silence at the vision in white gliding across the terrazzo on the arm of Santo Lazzari. For a moment, he wondered who the woman was—but he knew. He knew it in his bones, his blood. He knew it in his soul.

Holly Craig did not look like the Holly Craig he knew. The Holly Craig he preferred, he realized with a jolt. No, this Holly was sleek and lovely, with her blond hair piled on her head to reveal her elegant neck, and her body-hugging dress shimmering in the torches that were beginning to glow on the perimeter of the terrazzo.

She moved like liquid silk. And she clung to Santo Lazzari in a way that made him see red. Her hand rested easily on Santo's arm and her head was turned to gaze up at Santo as if he was the most wonderful thing she'd ever seen.

Drago wanted to rip her from the other man's grip and claim her as his in front of all these people. So no man would dare to touch her again.

Instead, he tamped down on the urge to fight and strode toward the laughing couple. Holly sobered instantly when she glanced over and saw him, but Santo continued to gaze down at her for a long minute before he looked up to meet Drago's gaze.

"*Grazie, bella mia*," Santo said as he took Holly's hand and kissed it. "It's been a pleasure talking with you."

"And you," she replied, her voice soft and sweet in a way it never was with him. With everyone else—Nicky, Sylvia, the passport clerk, a flight attendant—but never him. That thought grated on his mind as he took Holly's hand and gripped it tight.

"*Amore*," he said. "I have been waiting for you to arrive."

She smiled, but he knew it was false. "And here I am."

"Yes, here you are."

He wanted to drag her back inside and lock her in her room, but instead he turned and led her into the gathering. He introduced her to many people as they circulated. He made sure she had wine and food, and he kept her moored at his side. Much of the time, her hand was anchored in his, until he could concentrate only on that small area of skin where they touched. Until his senses were overrun with sensation and desire.

As soon as he could do so without drawing attention, he dragged her through another door and into his office. He closed the door behind them and turned to face her. She stood in the darkness, her dress catching the light from outside and shimmering like white flame. He closed the distance between them, until he stood before her, dominating her space.

Her scent stole to him and he stiffened as he finally realized what had puzzled him for the past hour. "You are not wearing Sky."

"No."

"Why not?"

"Because I'm doing everything else you want of me."

"Everything else is not quite as good as everything," he grated.

She shrugged. "I will wear it the next time."

His blood beat in his ears. "How do you know there will be a next time?"

That made her pause. "I don't."

"What were you talking to Santo about?"

She seemed taken aback. "We talked about many things. You, the campaign, the weather."

His eyes narrowed. "That's all?"

Her chin lifted in the darkness. "Why do you care, Drago? You aren't interested in me as anything more than a face for your campaign, so what does it matter what I talk about with another man?"

"You are the mother of my child."

"Oh, so that's important to you now? I thought I was an obstacle, a situation to be dealt with."

The truth of her words slid beneath his skin. "And I will deal with you, *cara mia*. Whatever you thought before you came here, whatever ideas you might have had, you can forget. Nicky is my son, and my heir, and I will not allow you to withhold him from me or to use him to control me. Are we clear?"

"You're disgusting, do you know that?" She flung the words like poisoned darts. "I'm sorry for whatever hell you might have gone through in your life, but I am not your mother and I won't abandon my son. You can't buy me off, and you can't make me go away. I'll fight you, Drago. I'll fight you to the bitter end, and I won't do it cleanly. If you force me, I'll take to the internet. Then I'll call the media and I'll smear you and Navarra Cosmetics from one end of this planet to the other."

Fury rose to a dull roar inside him—but there was something else, too. Excitement. He recognized it in the way his body quivered, the way his nerve endings twitched and tingled.

Every cell in his being was attuned to her, attuned to her softness, her scent, her heat. He suddenly wanted to touch her. He wanted to thrust inside her body, wanted to feel her cling to him, shape herself around him, gasp and moan and shudder beneath him as he made her come again and again.

He dragged himself back from the brink, back from that irretrievable moment when he would claim her mouth for his own and then not cease until he'd had her body, too.

"Try it," he said. "I have the money to make it go away."

He could employ an entire team to counteract anything she tried online or with the media.

Sure, all it took was a sound bite and the idea that powerful, wealthy Drago di Navarra was being unfair to this poor woman, and he could suffer some bad publicity. But he'd weathered bad publicity before. He wasn't afraid of it.

"Of course you do," she said. "That's how you operate, isn't it? You buy people off. You threaten and yell and order, and people do what you want. Well, not me, Drago. We have a contract, and don't think I won't take you to court if you break it."

He could have laughed if he weren't so angry. She had no idea how powerless she was. How he could tie her up in court until she had nothing left to battle him with. She would win, but she would have nothing once she paid her lawyers.

Suddenly, he was tired of this. He was tired of battling with her—of battling with himself—when what he really wanted was to have her beneath him. There was no reason he could think of to fight this attraction a moment longer.

He reached for her and she gasped. But then he tugged her in close, until their bodies were pressed tightly together, his fingers spread across the skin of her back where the dress dipped down. She was warm, and his fingers tingled as if electricity flowed beneath her skin.

"Your threat is as frightening as a swat from a kitten," he murmured, his gaze focusing on her lips—those lush, pretty lips that had dropped open in surprise.

Her head tilted back, her eyes searching his. The heat of her burned into him. His cock leaped against the confines of his trousers, and he knew she felt it by the widening of her eyes. She did not try to move away, and he experienced a surge of triumph. Her palms on his chest became fistfuls of his shirt. Her eyes filled with sexual heat.

Oh, yes, he'd not read this wrong at all. She wanted him. Desperately.

"I'm not a kitten, Drago," she said, her gaze on his mouth. "I mean what I say."

"Yes," he said, his hands sliding down her back, cupping her bottom and pulling her in closer to the heat and hardness of his body. "I know you do."

She gasped. And then she moved her hips. It was a slight movement, the whisper of an arch, but he knew in that moment that she was lost. As lost and helpless to this pull between them as he was.

"I hate you," she said, the sound halfway to a moan as he held her to him and slid the hardness of his body along the sensitive heart of her.

"Yes," he said. "You hate me, *bella mia*. I can feel it so strongly."

She gasped again. "This is so wrong," she said. "I shouldn't feel like this, not after the things you've said…."

Neither should he. But he lowered his head and slid his mouth along the sweet curve of her jaw anyway. Her fingers flexed convulsively in his shirt.

"Don't think, Holly. Just feel. Feel what we do to each other…."

CHAPTER ELEVEN

A CORNER OF Holly's brain told her she needed to stop this. That she needed to push this man away and let him know, once and for all, that she was not his to command.

But she couldn't do it. Because she was his. She wanted him to command her, at least in this. She wanted to feel his heat and hardness and strength. Wanted to lose herself in him, in the way he made her feel.

He confused her, and excited her. He frightened her, and challenged her. She hated him—and she wanted him. She'd spent the past hour trying to focus on the conversations around her, trying to smile and be the Sky spokesmodel, but all her senses kept coming back to one immutable fact: Drago's hand on hers was driving her insane.

Now she had much more than his hand. His mouth moved along her jaw, slid to her ear. He nibbled the tender flesh of her earlobe, and she could feel the erotic pull all the way to her toes. She'd long since passed the mark where she was ready for him. Her sex felt heavy between her thighs, achy. She was wet and hot. She *needed*.

She slipped her arms around his neck and he rewarded her with a lick of his tongue on the tender flesh behind her ear.

Then he growled something in Italian and his hands went to her waist. He found the zipper at her back and slid it down slowly, until the bodice of her strapless dress gaped. His fingers found the clasp of her bra and then her breasts were free from their confinement.

Holly instinctively covered herself. "There are people outside," she said in a panic. "They will notice we've gone."

"Yes, they will notice. But they won't search for us, *bella mia*. They are well fed, plied with the best wines and dishes I have to offer. They will stay and listen to the musicians, they will eat and drink and talk. They will not follow us."

She felt so wicked standing here in his office, naked from the waist up, and hearing the strains of music and voices coming from the gardens. Drago covered her hands with his, gently pulled them away until her breasts were bare and gooseflesh rose on her skin.

Then his palms found them, shaped them, and her heart shuddered in her chest.

"So lovely," he said. "So tempting."

And then he dropped his head and took one tight nipple in his mouth. Holly thought she would come unglued right then. She clutched his head, cried out with the sweet torture of his lips and tongue and teeth on her breast. She hadn't been touched like this in a year. Not since he'd been the one to show her how beautiful and perfect it could be.

"Drago," she gasped. "I don't know—"

"I do," he said. Then he pressed her breasts together in his hands, moved between them, licking and sucking her nipples while she arched her back and thrust them into his hot mouth. She felt every tug, every pull between her legs, as if her nipples were somehow attached to her sex.

He made her utterly crazy. She shouldn't be doing this, shouldn't be succumbing to the sensual power he had— but she didn't want to stop. It had been too long, and she'd been too lonely.

If he wanted her this way, if he couldn't help himself,

either, then maybe there was a chance for them. A chance they could work out their differences and be good parents to their child for his sake.

"I want to touch you," she cried at the next sweet spike of pleasure.

"Then touch me."

Holly shoved his tuxedo jacket from his shoulders, then tugged his shirt from his waistband. Her hands slipped beneath the fabric until her palms were—finally, finally—on his hot flesh. His skin quivered beneath her touch, and it made her bold.

She found his nipples, pinched them between her thumbs and forefingers while he sucked on hers. He groaned low in his throat. And then he pushed her back, ripped open his tie and shirt, studs scattering across the floor.

His chest was so perfect, so beautiful. He wasn't muscle-bound, like a body builder who didn't know when to quit. But he had a hard physique that made her mouth water. His eyes, when she finally dragged her gaze away from his firm pectorals, sizzled into her.

"Do you want me, Holly?"

She should tell him no. She knew she should, but she couldn't. She nodded mutely.

"Then come to me." He opened his arms and she went into them. When their skin touched, she wanted to moan with the pleasure. Drago's fingers roamed over her flesh, his thumbs gliding over her sensitive nipples again and again. Holly spread her hands on his chest, slid her fingers over the firm planes of muscle.

She looked up, into his eyes, her heart turning over at the heat she saw there. She wanted him to kiss her. It was odd to think he'd had his mouth on her breasts, but had not yet kissed her. She moved restlessly in his arms, stretched up on tiptoes to find his mouth, but he dropped his lips to the side of her neck again.

The fire between them spun up quickly. Drago pushed the dress down her hips until it pooled at her feet. "It will wrinkle," she said.

"I don't care."

She reached for his zipper. It didn't take her a moment to free him from his trousers. She wrapped her hand around his hot, hard flesh, her heart thrumming hard, making her dizzy.

His groan made her want to do things she'd never done before. She dropped to her knees and put her mouth around him, her tongue curling and gliding over his hot flesh.

Drago swore. She glanced up at him, and his eyes were closed tight. His jaw flexed as if he were in pain.

But she knew it wasn't pain—or not the bad kind, anyway.

Still, he didn't let her explore him the way she wanted. Too soon, he dragged her up into his arms and speared his hand into her hair. This time—oh, yes, this time—his mouth came down on hers.

And that was when she knew that nothing in her life would ever be the same again.

Holly's knees buckled when Drago's tongue touched hers. It was a silly reaction, and yet she couldn't control it. She'd forgotten just how drugging his kisses were. How necessary.

He caught her around the waist, and then he lifted her and turned until she was sitting on his desk. The wood was cold on her bare bottom. She was still wearing the lacy thong that went with the dress, but it didn't protect her skin from the coolness.

Not that she wanted to be protected. It was a welcome coolness, since the heat of their bodies threatened to incinerate her.

Drago tugged at her panties until she lifted her bottom and he could yank them off. Then he spread her knees wide and stepped between them. Instinctively, Holly curled her legs around his waist. Together, they fell backward—she heard the crash of many things hitting the floor and realized that Drago had swept them away with his arm as he'd laid her down on the desk. She only hoped there was nothing breakable—

And then she didn't care. Drago's mouth was thorough, demanding. His hard erection rode the seam of her body, gliding against her wetness with the most deliciously pleasurable friction imaginable.

It wasn't enough. She wanted more, wanted him inside her. Her hands kneaded the flesh of his back, skated down his sides, over his hips. She tried to reach between them, tried to guide him into her, but he pulled back with a muttered curse.

"Condom," he said. And then somehow he found one in the desk. He pulled away and rolled it on. She lay on the desk and watched him, feasted her eyes on the sheer beauty of his body. He put his hand over the mound of her sex, and she bit her lip to keep from crying out. Then he slid a finger down, into all that wetness. He hissed, as if she'd burned him—and then he skimmed over her damp skin while she whimpered.

Drago traced her, the plumpness on the outside, the delicate ridges on the inside, and all the while her heart beat a crazy rhythm in her chest. When he touched her most sensitive spot again, she cried out as sensation rocked her.

"You're so ready for me, *cara*," he said. "And it is everything I can do not to take what you offer right this very moment."

Her eyes snapped open. "Take it. Please."

He shook his head, and her heart dropped. Was this some crazy act of revenge? Was he going to deny this heat between them now that they'd come so far? Was he going to send her away before anything happened?

Disappointment tasted bitter. So bitter.

But then he spoke and her heart soared once more. "Not yet. First, I want to make you come." He stroked her again, and she shuddered. "I want you to sob my name, Holly. I want you to beg me for release."

"I'll beg now," she told him, her body on fire. "I have no shame."

And she didn't. Not where he was concerned. The only shame she'd ever felt was when he'd kicked her out. She'd not felt one moment of guilt for what she'd done with him. She might not have always realized that, but it was the truth. There was no shame in these feelings, no shame in this fire between them.

He laughed, a deep sensual purr that reverberated through her. "Patience, *cara*. Some things are worth the wait."

"I've been waiting a year," she said heatedly, and his eyes darkened. But it wasn't an angry darkening. No, instead she sensed he was on the edge of control. He was every bit as eager as she was. He just didn't want to admit it. Or perhaps it was better to say that Drago di Navarra was accustomed to being in control. Taking his time meant he could govern his need. Meant that he was superhuman, not prey to the usual vicissitudes of emotion.

But Holly wanted him to lose control. She didn't know why it was important to her, but if she was committed to doing this with him—and she was—she wanted it to be something he couldn't shape into what he wanted it to be. She wanted it to be as wild and chaotic for him as it was for her.

Holly lifted herself on her elbows and reached for him. His breath hissed in when she closed her hand around him. He was so hot and hard that she wondered how he could stand it.

Because she could barely stand the empty ache in her core. The only way to ease that ache was to fill it with him.

"I'm begging you now, Drago," she said, hardly recognizing the note of desperation in her voice. "I'm begging you."

His eyes darkened again. Then he lowered his head slowly, so slowly, that she thought he would deny her. But then he kissed her, his lips fusing with hers so sweetly and perfectly that she let go of him and wrapped her arms around his neck.

The kiss was hotter than any she'd ever experienced with him. He took her mouth completely, utterly, and she gave herself up to him as if she'd been born to do so. Her legs went around his waist again, locked tight to keep him from leaving her.

But he had no intention of doing so. He found her entrance—and then he slid inside her. Slowly, but surely. Exquisitely. Holly gasped at the fullness of his possession. She hadn't remembered it being this way before, but of course it had been.

She closed her eyes. No, it would have been somewhat more intense simply because she'd been a virgin. She was no longer a virgin, and while she had no experience of sex beyond that single night with Drago, she was more than ready for this moment.

Drago groaned as he seated himself fully inside her. "Look at me, *bella*."

Holly opened her eyes again, met the intensity of his hot stare. The look on his face made her stomach flip. He was so intense, so beautiful. And, for this moment at least, he was hers.

"You excite me, Holly. You make me…"

Whatever he was going to say was lost as he closed his eyes and gripped her hips. His head tilted back, the muscles in his neck cording tight. And then he shifted his hips, withdrawing almost completely before slamming into her again.

Holly licked her lips as sensation bloomed in her core. A moment later, Drago was there, sucking her tongue into his mouth. She wrapped her arms around him and held on tight while he held her hips in two broad hands and pumped into her again and again.

She'd forgotten how amazing it was between them. How incredible. How necessary. The tension in her body wound tighter and tighter—until finally it snapped and flung her out over infinite space.

She fell forever, her body shuddering and trembling as she cried out her pleasure. Her senses were so keen, so sharp. She could smell their passion, a combination of flame and sweat and sex, and she could smell the flowers in the garden, the wine, the food, the mingled perfumes of dozens of people.

But, mostly, she smelled him—sandalwood, pears, moss and man. He was warm and hard and vibrant, and he owned her body in this moment.

When she thought she would never move again, when she was boneless and liquid in his arms, he withdrew from her body. And then he turned her so that she was sprawled over the desk, her bottom in the air, her breasts pressed against the wood.

She spread her arms and gripped either edge of the desk as Drago entered her again. It was different this time, though just as delicious. The pressure was exquisite as he stroked into her. She didn't think she could come again but he slid his hand around her body, found her sweet spot. Holly moaned and bucked against him as the spring began to tighten once more.

Too quickly, she shattered, coming in a hot, hard rush of feeling that left her limp and weak.

Drago rocked into her body again and again—and then

he stiffened. Her name was a broken groan in his throat. A moment later, his lips settled on her shoulder and a shiver went through her. He was still inside her, still hard. She tilted her hips up, and Drago gasped.

"*Dio*, Holly. What you do to me should be illegal."

She couldn't help but laugh, though it didn't sound like her usual laugh. No, this was the laugh of a sensual woman. A satisfied woman. It was low and sexy and sultry. She liked it. "Maybe it is illegal," she said. "Maybe I like it that way."

He withdrew from her body and helped her up, turning her until they were pressed together from breast to hip. Her heart beat hard, dizzily. Drago tilted her chin up with a finger and kissed her thoroughly.

Then he broke the kiss and pressed his forehead to hers. "I'm taking you to bed, Holly. *My* bed. Any complaints?"

She thought about the party in the garden, about her baby tucked away in his room, and about the man standing before her. "Not a single one," she said.

Drago grinned. "This is what I like to hear."

"Obedience?" she asked as she searched for her underwear in the darkened room. But she said it teasingly for once.

He laughed. "In this instance, absolutely." He came over and helped her into her dress, his mouth dropped to her shoulder as he slid her zipper up again. "But I promise to make it worth your while, *amore mia*."

Drago awoke in that early hour before dawn. Something felt different, and it took him a moment of lying there in the darkness and processing everything to realize what it was.

He was happy.

He frowned. But he shouldn't be happy. Not at all.

He should be murderously angry with the woman lying beside him. He had been angry. Violently so. But then he'd lost himself in her body and he hadn't been the same since. He couldn't seem to dredge up the fury he'd felt earlier. All he had now was hurt and sadness and desire. Plenty of desire.

Dio, what they'd done to each other last night. He was worn-out, sated. He couldn't remember the last time he'd felt so utterly drained after sex. Except, perhaps, the last time he'd been with her.

Drago threw the covers back and got out of bed. Quietly, so as not to wake Holly. She lay on her side, curled up, with her buttocks thrust toward him.

He had an urge to lean down and nip her.

Drago resolutely turned away from the woman in his bed and tugged on a pair of jeans he'd thrown over a chair when he'd been changing into his tuxedo. He had no idea when the party had ended or when the last guest had left. He was confident, however, they'd had a good time, regardless of his absence.

He left the room and padded down to the nursery, which was a few doors away on the same corridor. He'd originally planned to put Holly and her baby in another wing of the house—until he'd discovered the truth about the child.

Now the baby was his son and he had no idea what that meant to him other than it meant something important. He stepped into the nursery and walked over to the crib. The boy lay on his back, eyes closed, little chest rising and falling evenly.

Drago stood there and gazed down at the sleeping child while an emotional tornado whirled inside his soul. This was *his* flesh, *his* blood. He could see it now. In the dark hair, in the shape of the mouth, in the impossibly long lashes. This child was stamped with the Di Navarra signature traits like a piece of fine art was signed by the maker.

He felt a rush of feeling in his gut. He wanted to pick the boy up and hold him, but of course he wasn't about to do so. Even if he knew what he was doing, he didn't want to wake the baby when he slept so peacefully.

Drago might not know much about babies, but he knew they didn't sleep on command or at the convenience of others. If this one was asleep now, best to leave him that way. He watched the boy and thought of his own mother. Had she ever stood over him and felt this rush of emotion and protectiveness like he felt right now?

Probably not. What he didn't understand was how she couldn't feel those things. He didn't even know this child, not really, and he already knew he would never allow anyone to harm this baby. Not ever.

His eyes stung with tears. It stunned him, but he wiped them away and stood there a moment longer, clutching the sides of the crib and watching Nicky's little mouth move in his sleep. So beautiful. So perfect.

When he finally turned to leave, he drew up short. Holly stood in the doorway, her long reddish-blond hair hanging in disarray over her shoulders and down her back. She was bare-legged, having slipped into his discarded shirt. She looked so fresh and pretty, so innocent and sensual all at once.

Something twisted in his chest. He wanted to grab her and hold her close, but he didn't act on the urge.

"How is he?" she whispered.

"Asleep."

Holly glided over to his side and gazed down at her son. A smile curved the corners of her mouth and Drago felt a strong desire to kiss her. To own her and own that smile, too.

"He's so sweet," she said softly. "A very good baby." Then she looked up at him, and his heart clenched at the sadness on her face. It surprised him how much she affected him. How much he wanted to protect her and their baby, too.

He'd never felt this kind of possessiveness toward any-one. He knew it was because his feelings for her were all tangled up with the knowledge he'd fathered this child, but he couldn't quite seem to separate them.

He'd told her to walk away earlier. To take his money and walk away.

Now he couldn't imagine letting her go. He didn't *want* to let her go. And that frightened him.

Her brows drew together as she reached up and ran her hand along his jaw. "Don't worry," she said, and he knew that some of what he was feeling must have shown on his face. "You'll be fine with him. He will love you to pieces."

His heart seized. "I'm sure you're right," he said.

She slipped her arms around his waist and laid her head on his chest. "I am right. You'll see. Everything will be perfect."

He wanted to believe it, but he'd learned a long time ago that nothing was perfect.

CHAPTER TWELVE

TIME WAS FLUID. It moved like a river, rolling smoothly and inexorably forward. Sometimes there were rocks. Sometimes there weren't.

Holly sighed and looked up from her work. There had been no rocks for days now. She liked it this way. Life with Drago had been one long, immensely pleasurable ride along smooth water these past two weeks.

The days were pleasant—she played with Nicky, read books and mixed her perfumes. Drago had supplied her with everything she needed, just as he'd promised. He worked from home much of the time, though sometimes he got up early and took a helicopter to his office in Rome. She missed him when he wasn't at the house. Because when he was, he often came searching for her in the middle of the day.

They'd made frantic love against the wall of a closet once. He'd come looking for her and found her heading for her workroom. Instead of leading her back to the room they shared, he'd opened the nearest door—a closet—and dragged her inside. It had been incredibly erotic, fumbling with their clothes among the linens, mouth seeking mouth. He'd had to put his hand over her mouth to stop her cries when he'd buried himself deep inside her, their bodies sweating and writhing as they'd flown toward that perfect release. She'd bitten him, and he'd laughed.

There were other times, too, wonderful times, when they retreated to their room in the middle of the day and made love while the world moved by outside. She loved those moments, when it seemed as if they were the only two people who existed.

But of course she loved it when Drago came to play with Nicky, too. He'd been wary at first, nervous, but now he was a natural. And Nicky loved him, laughing whenever Drago picked him up and swooped him around the room, pretending he was a bird or a superhero.

She laughed, too, loving the sound of her two men enjoying each other's company.

But, as perfect as life had been lately, she wasn't worry-free. She and Drago avoided discussing anything to do with the future. What happened now?

She had no idea, and it worried her. For all her bravery, there were certain things she still couldn't manage to be vocal about. And the future was one of them.

There had been delays on the Sky campaign, so she'd told herself to stop thinking about it. Instead, she spent time working on her scents.

She tested the latest batch of Colette. Then she leaned back, satisfied it was perfect. She'd given some to the maids, and then she'd given some to the cook when she'd expressed an interest. Several of Drago's staff were now wearing her fragrances, not his. If he'd noticed, he hadn't said anything.

And she didn't think he could help but notice, since she wore the same fragrance herself. Colette was light, fresh and floral. There was lavender, verbena, vanilla, and a few secrets she wouldn't divulge to anyone. But it was unmistakable, and it tended to flatter most body chemistries. No one had been unable to wear it yet.

She sniffed the tester again, closing her eyes as she did so. It made her think of home, of Gran's lovely face. Of the fat blooms in Gran's garden, and the delicious gumbo on Gran's stove. She missed Gran so much.

A tear fell and she dashed it away, sniffling. She was happy, dammit. Happy.

She had a wonderful baby and a man she loved—

Holly froze. *Love?* How could she love Drago di Navarra? What they had was hot, physical and addictive. It was also volatile and chaotic in many ways.

But it wasn't emotional. It was sex.

When it was over, she could walk away and not miss a thing....

Holly hung her head as a sharp pain carved into her at the thought. Oh, dear heaven, it *was* emotional. For her anyway. Because the thought of leaving Drago, of not being a part of his life anymore, felt as if she were trying to slice off an arm or leg. She couldn't imagine life without him. Didn't want to.

That didn't mean it was love, though. He was the father of her baby, and it was inevitable she felt something tender for him, especially as they spent time together and as he doted on his son. In spite of his childhood, in spite of a mother who'd given him up and made him feel unloved, he was capable of so much love when it came to his little boy.

But what about her? How did he feel about her?

"Holly."

She turned at the sound of his voice, her heart leaping. A single tear spilled down her cheek and she hurriedly wiped it away.

"What's wrong?" he said, coming over to her side and kneeling down. He looked so concerned, and her heart turned over.

"I was thinking of Gran," she said huskily. It was true.

He reached up and wiped away another tear that escaped. "I'm sorry you lost her, Holly."

She shrugged, though she felt anything but lighthearted at the moment. "That's life, right?"

He stood and pulled her into his arms. She went willingly, burying her head against his chest and breathing him in. Oh, how she loved the smell of him. He wasn't wearing cologne today, but he still smelled like pears to her. Not sweet, but not tart, either. Delicious and crisp and inviting. That was Drago.

"It is life, but that doesn't make it hurt any less."

They stood that way for a long while, and then she pushed back and looked up at him, smiling through her tears. "I'm fine, Drago. I just miss her sometimes."

He took her hand and led her out onto the terrace. They sank onto a settee that was shaded from the sun by a vine-covered arbor. Fat grapes hung down, waiting for someone to pick them.

"Tell me about her," he commanded. She would have laughed at his imperious tone if she weren't touched by his desire to make her feel better.

"She raised me. I told you that before. I never knew my father, and my mother died when I was young. Gramps had died years before, so it was just me and Gran in her little cottage. She grew so many things, Drago. Vegetables, herbs and flowers. We ate well and we made essences. I had a wonderful childhood. I never thought I was missing out on anything."

"And then she died, and you couldn't keep her home."

She nodded. "Gran didn't have insurance, so when she got sick with cancer she had to borrow against the house. She didn't want to do it at first, but she really had no choice. And I was positive we'd find a way, once she was cured, to pay the money back."

She sucked in a pained breath. "But she wasn't cured, and I didn't find a way. After I buried her, there was hardly anything left. The cottage was repossessed. Someone else lives there now." She swallowed a fresh load of tears, her emotions whirling. "I just hope they love it the way I did."

His thumb skated rhythmically over the back of her hand. "I don't think they can, Holly. But I bet they love it in their own way."

Her throat was tight with emotion. He'd put it so perfectly. "Yes, I'm sure you're right. It would be impossible not to appreciate its beauty. The house isn't very big, but Gran had an acre of land and all of it planted and carefully tended. The wife was a gardener, so I'm sure she's in heaven with all the plants."

One of the maids came outside then and asked if they'd like something to drink. Drago asked for a bottle of wine and some water. Holly could smell the scent of Colette in the air. Drago watched the maid walk away.

"Don't think I haven't noticed that everyone smells similar to you," he said mildly.

She shrugged. "I was certain you must have. Are you angry?"

He laughed. "No one who works here is required to wear Navarra products, *cara*. For all I know, the housekeeper mixes up her own scents in her kitchen."

"She might, but that's not what she's wearing right now," Holly said.

"It's…different. I assume it's your Colette?"

Joy washed through her. "Yes. Gran and I made it together."

He looked thoughtful. "I think I like it. It's fresh, not overwhelming. Floral, but not cloying."

Holly nodded eagerly. "Yes, that's it exactly. I haven't found a woman yet whose body chemistry didn't complement the fragrance. It's different on everyone, but the same, too. If that makes sense."

He laughed. "You are talking to a man who hears a hundred different pitches a week for things that are the same but different. Sometimes it makes sense. Often, it's—how do you Americans say it?—bullshit."

"And is it bullshit this time?"

He pursed his lips in thought. "Perhaps not. But I will need more information." His gaze slid down her body, back up again, and she tingled everywhere he looked. "I will need a thorough, *private* demonstration, Holly Craig."

"I think I can arrange that," she told him. "Let me speak to the research-and-development department. I'll get back with you."

His eyes sparkled. "Mmm, and if I'm unwilling to wait that long?"

She tipped her head to the returning maid. "I think you must, Mr. Di Navarra. Your wine has arrived."

"Ah, but wine is portable," he said with a wink.

Drago was gone the next morning when Holly woke, off to Rome to tend to his business. She lay in the bed alone and thought about everything that had happened these past few weeks. She was happier than she'd have ever thought she could be, and she was frightened, too.

Drago did not talk about the future. Not ever. She had no idea what she meant to him, if anything. Oh, sure, they were lovers and she was the mother of his child—but what did that mean to him, beyond the here and now? He seemed to need her as much as she needed him—but he never said any tender words, never talked about what the future might hold for them.

She was under contract for a year, but only if the test shots went well. So far, there had been no test shots. There had been no shoot. Drago said it took time to do what he wanted and not to worry, but she worried nevertheless.

He did things like ask her about Gran and express his sorrow for her loss, and she wondered endlessly if that meant he felt something. Or if he was just being polite.

Yesterday, he'd said he'd needed more information about Colette. But once they'd been alone, perfume had been the furthest thing from his mind. He'd stripped her naked and made her mindless with pleasure. But when it was over, when they were sated and lying together in the bed, he'd pulled her close and fallen asleep. He'd not asked her one question about her fragrance.

She'd told herself it was ridiculous to be disappointed, especially after the way he'd held her and caressed her and wrung every drop of pleasure from her body, but she couldn't help herself. She wanted to be taken seriously, and Drago only wanted to use her body.

Not that she minded that part. But she wanted more. She wanted to know he thought about more than having sex with her. And she wanted to know what would happen when the campaign was over. Or if he didn't like the test shots and it never began.

He had to know she'd meant what she said about not giving up Nicky. But he had so much money and power. Did he really care what she said? He could fight her for custody. He might even win.

Holly's heart squeezed tight. She couldn't let that happen.

She flung the covers back and went to take a shower. After, she dressed in jeans and a T-shirt and went to find Sylvia and Nicky. They were in the garden, and Holly went to join them, her heart swelling with love for her baby. He sat on a blanket in the shade, playing with his toys, while Sylvia read a book. When he saw her coming, he threw the toy and began babbling excitedly. His little arms stretched up to her, and Holly bent to pick him up.

"Hello, precious," she said, sticking her nose against his neck and breathing in his soft baby scent.

She greeted Sylvia warmly, though she was still wary

of having anyone else take care of her son. It felt as if he wasn't hers as much, and she knew that was silly, but since Gran had died, she'd been so alone in the world with no other family. She had Gabi, of course, but Gabi didn't share DNA with her. This little guy, however, had become her world. She couldn't lose him. Not ever.

Holly spent the rest of the morning with Nicky and Sylvia, and then she put Nicky down for his nap and went to the room set up with her supplies. She had an idea for something new that she wanted to play with. When she'd been sitting in the grass earlier, the scent of sun-warmed cherries had seemed to waft over her from nowhere. They combined with the scent of the grapes in the arbor and the grass and soil beneath her to make her think of summer afternoons. It didn't mean she would get anything out of combining essences, but it was fun to play.

And it kept her mind occupied.

Sometime during the afternoon, there was a knock at her door. Her heart skipped when she thought it might be Drago, but then she realized he usually strode in without knocking.

"Yes," she called, and a maid opened the door.

"Signorina," she said, "there is a man here to see you."

Holly blinked. "Me? Are you certain?"

"Sí. It is Signore Lazzari, and he says he wishes to speak to you."

She hadn't thought about Santo Lazzari in two weeks, so to have him here now was a bit of a surprise. Still, she didn't have any reason not to see him. He knew she was the new face of Sky, and he was one of Drago's business associates.

"I'll be there in a minute," she said.

The maid inclined her head and left. Holly stoppered her essences, made a few quick notes and then went out to greet Santo.

* * *

Drago sat at his desk in his office in Rome and tried to concentrate on the numbers in front of him. But he couldn't seem to focus. He kept coming back to Holly, to the way she clung to him, the way she felt beneath him when their bodies were joined, the way he felt inside when he was with her.

She made him want to be a better man. She made him want to try to open his heart and trust someone. He'd never trusted anyone, not since he was little and had learned he could rely only on himself. That he was responsible for his own well-being instead of the woman who should have been taking care of him. He'd never had that freedom other kids had had, that freedom to play and have fun and not *think* about survival and belonging.

He'd always had to think about those things. About his place in his mother's world, and his place in the world at large. He had always been worth a lot of money. He still was, even more so now that he was in charge of it. His money enticed people to try to use him for their own purposes, to try to chip off just a little bit for themselves.

Holly had had his child, but she hadn't tried to get money from him. She hadn't shown up on his doorstep, threatening him with a paternity suit, threatening him with selling her story to the tabloids if he didn't pay up. She'd never tried to use Nicky to get anything from him.

She had kept him secret, though. And she had kept that knowledge hidden while she'd negotiated for a contract with him. She said it was because she wanted to secure her child's future. Because she was afraid he would kick her out again.

If he were honest with himself, she'd had every reason to think he might do just that.

He had not handled her betrayal quite so well the first time. In fact, he'd reacted in a way he never did. Blindly, emotionally. He'd thrown her out instead of listening to her pitch, politely telling her "no, thanks," and then sending her on her way.

But she'd blindsided him. Or, rather, his own feelings had blindsided him. In a single moment, Holly Craig had reminded him what it had felt like to be worth nothing as a person and everything as an entity. He'd hated her for making him feel that way.

And how did he feel now?

Drago sighed. That was the problem. He didn't know. He only knew that since taking her to his bed, he'd felt a sense of relief and joy that he hadn't experienced in a very long time. It made no sense, especially when he considered that she'd lied to him for so long—but maybe he was tired of being suspicious, tired of letting the past dictate the future.

He had a child with her, a wonderful, adorable child. And he wanted that child to have the things he hadn't had: a stable home, a father, love. Holly loved Nicky, and he loved Nicky. Shouldn't they work together to give their boy everything they could?

They hadn't had the best beginning, but they could have a good future together. All he had to do was take a chance. It took him a few more hours of thinking and considering and weighing all the options, but in the end he made a decision.

He picked up the phone and started to make a few calls. When he got home tonight, he would take the first step toward the future.

CHAPTER THIRTEEN

EXCITEMENT BUBBLED AND popped in Holly's veins like fine champagne poured into a crystal flute. Santo Lazzari wanted her to make perfume for House of Lazzari. He wanted to buy Colette. It was everything she'd ever dreamed, everything she'd wanted when she and Gran had been mixing their blends together—and then, after, when Gran was gone and Holly had been determined to save her home and introduce the world to Gran's perfume.

But there was also an undercurrent of sadness in her joy. Drago. She'd wanted *him* to want Colette. She'd wanted him to be the one who was excited about the possibilities, who praised her for her skill and who mapped out a potential campaign that showed what he could do with her fragrance.

Except, he didn't seem interested. Yesterday, she'd thought he finally would talk to her about it, but he'd kissed her instead. And then he'd taken her to bed and made love to her and all thoughts of perfume had flown out the window.

Now she stood in her workroom and waited for him to return from Rome. She'd told Santo she had to think about it overnight, but what she really wanted to know was how Drago felt. Did he want Colette? Or was that nothing more than a dead end?

Finally, when the shadows grew long on the tall pencil

pines, she heard the *whop-whop* of the rotors as Drago's helicopter returned. Her heart lodged in her throat as she went outside to greet him. He came walking up from the helipad, clad in a custom suit and handmade loafers, carrying a briefcase and looking lost in thought.

She watched him for a long moment, her breath catching at the sheer masculine beauty of him. Santo Lazzari was handsome, and he'd even flirted with her a little bit, but she'd been unmoved. When Drago walked across a room—or a lawn—she felt as if she were slowly burning up from the inside out. Every sense attuned to him. Every cell of her body ached for him.

He saw her, finally. His expression grew serious and her blood slowed to a crawl in her veins. What was he thinking?

"Holly," he said when he drew near. And then, before she could ask him what was on his mind, he dropped the briefcase and dragged her into his arms. He kissed her thoroughly, completely, until she was boneless in his embrace.

"I have something for you," he said when he finally lifted his head. His eyes sparked with heat and passion, and a throbbing ache set up shop in her core.

"I think I know what it is," she said teasingly, her heart thrumming fast.

He laughed. "I doubt it." Then he reached into his pocket and pulled out a small velvet box.

Holly's heart lodged in her throat. "What is it?"

"Open it."

No one had ever given her jewelry—and certainly not something in a velvet box. She knew the size, the shape, knew what it usually meant in commercials and movies. But what did it mean here?

Her hands stayed anchored at her sides as the world spun crazily around her. "I don't think I can."

He stood there so tall and handsome in the golden light. She could hear birds in the trees now that the helicopter was gone again. Inside the house, she heard the clink of dishes and knew the chef was preparing dinner. Drago's scent assailed her nostrils, along with the freshness of the evening breeze and the dampness of an approaching storm.

She felt everything so keenly, and she was afraid to move beyond this moment. Afraid it wouldn't mean what she wanted it to mean. Afraid it would end and she'd be brokenhearted again.

"Then I will do it for you," he said, flipping back the lid as he stood so close to her she could feel his heat enveloping her senses.

The ring wasn't huge by billionaire standards, but it was undoubtedly bigger than anything she'd ever thought she would have. And it was unmistakably an engagement ring. The center diamond was at least three carats, and the band held more diamonds, which enhanced the center and made it sparkle all the more. She didn't think the setting was white gold. Platinum most likely, unless there were a more rare metal she didn't know about.

"Marry me, Holly," he said. "We'll make a home for Nicky, and one day he'll inherit all of this."

Her chest ached as tears filled her eyes. "I don't know what to say."

He looked uncertain for a moment, as if he hadn't anticipated that answer. "Say yes."

She wanted to. Desperately. But she couldn't until she asked a question. He'd never given any indication of his feelings, and she needed to know. "Do you love me, Drago?"

He swallowed. "I care about you," he said, and her heart fell slowly, so slowly, until it hit the floor and shattered into a million pieces.

She told herself it was silly to feel sad or disappointed.

It was too soon to ask for more. He was proposing to her. Offering to make a home for Nicky, to give him a family. She knew how important that was to him. A man who'd never had a stable home life until he was nearly a teenager.

What more could she ask for right this moment? It was a start. And yet she was more hurt by his offer than cheered. She wanted *more*. She wanted him to feel the way she felt. She wanted him to feel as if he would burst trying to contain all these hot, bright feelings inside the shell of his skin, and she wanted him to care about the things she cared about.

She told herself this was enough, for now. But it wasn't.

"Santo Lazzari wants to buy Colette," she said on a whisper, because she couldn't say the other things she was thinking. She couldn't put her heart on the line when she was more and more certain he didn't feel the same way.

Drago's face changed. She watched the emotions crossing his features and knew she'd said the wrong thing. There was disbelief, hurt, loneliness and, finally, fury. He snapped the box closed and she jumped at the finality of the sound.

"And what does Lazzari have to do with this, Holly?" he gritted. "With what I am asking you right now? Are you hoping for a better offer from *him*?"

Shock hit her like a lightning bolt sizzling across a clear blue sky. "What? No! But you said you care about me, and this is something I care about. And you haven't spoken of it, though I keep waiting—"

His expression grew darker, if that were possible, more thunderous. His lips curled back from his teeth and she shrank away from him. "You think mentioning Lazzari to me will make me buy your perfume?" He held up the box in his clenched fist. His knuckles were white where he gripped it so hard. "I'm offering you more than you could have ever dreamed possible—money, position, even power—and you still care about your trite little scents?"

His words stabbed into her. *Trite little scents.* He thought her dreams were beneath his notice. No, he thought she wanted to make perfume only so she could make money. That she was driven by ambition and greed rather than joy and love.

He didn't really know her if he thought that. He'd spent these past few weeks with her, and he had no idea who she was. It hurt more than she'd ever thought possible.

Blindly, she turned away from him. Everything was blurry as she started across the terrace. She had to get away, or scream.

"Where are you going?" he thundered. "Holly? Holly!"

She didn't turn around. She didn't stop. She kept going until she was inside her room, the door locked to the outside. Until she could cry for everything she'd lost, and everything she would never have.

Drago went back to Rome. When he reached his apartment, he slammed inside and threw his briefcase on the couch. And then he took the velvet box from his trousers, where it had sat like a hard lump of marble, and wanted to howl in frustration.

He'd misjudged her again. He'd thought she wanted him, wanted this life, but she wanted him to buy her perfume and she didn't mind using Santo Lazzari to get him to do it. And she wanted him to proclaim his love for her, as if that would make a difference somehow.

Love. *Dio*, what kind of fool would love her?

Drago raked a hand through his hair. He didn't understand love. He didn't understand how anyone could let go enough to feel love. In his mind, it was a dangerous emotion that made people unstable. When you loved someone, you gave them the keys to your soul. The means with which to destroy you.

He'd spent years loving a mother who hadn't loved him back—or hadn't loved him enough. It had taken him years to get over the neglect, and he was not about to open himself up for that kind of experience ever again.

Holly knew, damn her. She *knew* how hard this was for him, how damaged a life he'd had. She knew and she insisted on pushing him.

Santo Lazzari. *Christo!* It had been only a few weeks, and they hadn't even begun the Sky shoot yet. Already she was scheming to get her perfume in front of another company. It infuriated him that she would betray him, that she would talk to Santo instead of to him.

Why hadn't she just asked him what he thought? Why hadn't she come to him instead of going behind his back?

The answer was obvious: because she didn't trust him.

Hot feelings swirled inside him. He wanted to punch something. Wanted to rage and howl and ask why he wasn't good enough for her.

He went over to the liquor cabinet and poured a shot of whiskey. His fingers shook as he poured and he stopped, stared at them. *Why wasn't he good enough for her?*

That was the kind of question he'd asked as a child. It was a question for his mother, not for Holly. He set the whiskey down and stared at a window across the street, a little lower than his. A man and woman danced together, the woman smiling up at him, the man saying something that made her smile.

Holly was not his mother. And she very likely hadn't gone to Santo. He remembered Santo escorting her onto the terrace a couple of weeks ago. Santo could have asked her about the scent she was wearing then. And she would have told him the truth.

And even if she'd pitched it herself, why should that matter to him?

If he were truthful with himself, he hadn't shown much interest, though he knew she worked hard on her fragrances. He'd been in the room she'd set up as a work area, he'd smelled her concoctions and he'd seen her notes. She was a professional. And she was good.

But he'd never told her that. *Why not?*

Drago stood in the darkness of his Rome apartment, with the city sounds wafting up from below and the lights of Rome's ancient ruins and sacred domes glittering before him, and felt more alone than he'd ever felt in his life.

What was he doing? Why was he here instead of back at his villa, with his beautiful son?

And with Holly.

A cold, sinking feeling started in his gut, spread through his limbs. What if he'd ruined it this time? What if he'd gone too far? He tried to imagine his life without her in it. Emptiness engulfed him.

It was more emptiness than he'd ever thought he could feel. Somehow, she had become important to him. To his life. If he had to live without her in it, how could he ever laugh again?

He was a fool. A blind fool, driven by things that had happened to him over twenty years ago instead of by the things that his life had become. Inside, he was still lost and alone and frightened. And he was waiting—waiting for betrayal. He expected it, looked for it, congratulated himself when it happened. Because it was what he knew was supposed to happen to him.

But what if it wasn't? What if the problem was all him? What if Holly was exactly what she seemed to be? A somewhat naive, trusting woman who'd had to learn how to survive on her own when she'd found herself pregnant and alone.

Drago turned away from the window, panic bubbling up from a well inside him that he'd kept capped for far too long. He was an idiot. And not for the reasons he'd supposed. No one had made him into a fool. He'd done it all by himself.

Holly woke in the middle of the night, her eyes swollen, her throat aching, and knew she had to leave. There could be no Sky. There could be no Drago. She would do whatever it took to arrange for him to see his son, but right now Nicky belonged to her and she wasn't leaving here without him.

She dressed in the dark, tossed some things into a bag and went to gather Nicky from his crib. Somehow she managed to get him into his carrier without waking him, and then she crept down the stairs and stood in the empty foyer, undecided about what to do. On the hall table, there were several sets of car keys in a box. She took one—a BMW—and went out to the garage.

It took her nearly forty-five minutes to get the car, find the nearest train station on the GPS and drive to it. She could have gone to the airport, but for now she figured she'd get a train to Rome, call Santo Lazzari and arrange to meet with him about Colette, and then get a one-way ticket back to Louisiana. If she could just get an advance, she'd be all right. She had some money, but not enough to get her very far.

Holly purchased a ticket to Rome and went to sit on a bench. She studied her ticket and studied the boards, hoping she'd found the right track. Her eyes were gritty and tired, and she suddenly just wanted to go back to sleep. Nicky stirred in his carrier, but he was too sleepy to wake just yet. She prepared a bottle and hoped it would keep him quiet once he did.

Eventually, her train arrived—or she hoped it was her train—and she boarded it, finding a seat in a corner and leaning her head against the window. It throbbed with the remnants of her crying fit, and the early-morning coolness felt good against her skin.

She dozed a bit and then the train lurched and started to glide down the tracks. Her heart ached with such a profound sadness that she could hardly acknowledge it. How could she go back to the life she'd left behind? How could she forget Drago this time?

The last time, she hadn't been in love with him—or maybe she had, but it had been so easy to convince herself she hated him instead. This time, her heart mourned for everything that could never be. They would see each other again. Because of Nicky. She couldn't get out of it and she didn't want to.

But she would have to figure out how to survive those moments when she had to face him for the sake of their child.

The train lurched again, and then began to slow. They hadn't quite made it out of the station when it stopped completely. The Italians on board seemed unperturbed about it all, but her pulse hummed along a little bit faster. She just wanted to get away, before Drago discovered she was gone. She figured she had time, since he'd presumably returned to Rome last night, but she was nervous nevertheless.

There was a commotion in the car behind her, raised voices, and she turned to look along with the other passengers. Her heart seemed to stop beating then. She could see Drago's face, determined and hard, and her legs turned to mush. She reached for her bag, slid out of her seat and grabbed the carrier. She was on her way down the car when the door behind her opened and a man shouted her name.

She spun, her hair whirling into her face, and confronted him—because there was no escape now.

"Go away, Drago," she said. "Just leave me alone."

He looked wild-eyed as he moved into the car. The

other passengers glanced between them with interest, eyes bouncing back and forth as if they were at a tennis match.

"Holly, please." He held his hand out, and she saw that it shook. She steeled her heart against him and shook her head. What a good actor he was.

"Stop it," she said coldly. "You're only pretending so these people won't think you're some kind of unfeeling monster. But we both know the truth, don't we?"

He looked taken aback. "No, that's not true." He tried to smile, but it wasn't a very good attempt. "Besides, since when do I care what anyone else thinks about me?"

He had a point there, but if she allowed it to penetrate, her shield would crumble. She had to be strong. For her baby. For herself.

"You don't care about anyone."

He took another step forward, one hand out in supplication. "I care about you."

Panic bloomed in her soul. "You don't. You're only saying that because I tried to leave. Well, guess what, Drago, you can't force me to stay! I won't prevent you from being a part of Nicky's life, but I won't stay here and let you ruin my life, either."

His hand dropped to his side. "I don't want to ruin your life, Holly. I want to make it better."

She laughed bitterly. "By locking me up in a gilded cage? By not trusting me? By belittling my dreams and my interests? By telling me I'll never be good enough for the likes of you?"

His expression was stark. And then he said something that stunned her. "You're too good for me, Holly. I'm the one who isn't good enough."

Anger seeped from her like air from a balloon. Confusion took up residence in her brain. She wanted to believe him, but how could she? "Is this a trick?"

He shook his head, and she finally saw that lost, lonely

man that lurked inside him. "It's not a trick. I'm a fool, Holly. I need you too much, and it scares me."

Holly stared at him for a long moment, studying his face. Her heart thundered and her blood pounded and her skin felt hot and tight.

"I think he tells the truth," a woman said, and Holly glanced over at her. She was a pretty woman, with dark hair and eyes shiny with tears. "It is *amore, signorina*."

Holly's heart skipped. "Is that true, Drago? Do you love me? Or is this all an elaborate ruse to get me to go back with you so you can take our son away?"

He stood there before her, so tall and commanding— and then he drew in a sharp breath and she heard the pain in it.

"I don't know what love is, Holly. I loved my mother. I know I did, and yet she didn't seem to care. She left me. I meant nothing at all to her. What if I am incapable of love? Of being loved?"

There was a huge lump in her throat. "You aren't incapable of being loved."

His eyes were filled with so much pain. "How do you know?"

She felt a tear spill over, and then another. How could she let him think such a thing when she knew the truth?

"Because I love you." The words felt like razor blades coming up, but once they were free, she was glad she'd said them.

She didn't know what would happen, but he moved then, an inexorable wave coming for her. Then he swept her up in his arms, her and Nicky, and held them tight, burying his face against her neck.

"I don't know what love is," he said, his voice a broken whisper in her ear. "But if it's this feeling that I would die without you, then yes, I love you. If you leave me, Holly, I will be more alone than I've ever been in my life."

The tears flowed freely down her cheeks now, and the train's inhabitants clapped and cheered.

"I want to stay with you, Drago. But I'm afraid. You hurt me, and I'm afraid."

His grip didn't ease. "I know. I've been an ass, Holly. I want you to come home with me, and I want you to marry me. And I want Colette, and whatever other perfume you want to make for me. I want you to be happy, to do what you love—and I'm sorry I said it was trite. It's not. Nothing you do is trite. I was just…afraid."

Holly drew in a shaky breath. And then she pulled back and put her hand on his cheek—his beloved cheek—and caressed him. "I love you, Drago. You can't make me stop. It has nothing to do with your money or your stupid cosmetics company. Even if you had nothing, I would love you."

He wiped away the tears on her cheeks with shaky fingers. His eyes shimmered with moisture, though he grinned to try to hide it. "That's a pretty speech, considering I am worth somewhere in the neighborhood of eighty billion dollars. It's easy to love a rich man, *amore mia*."

She laughed then. "Perhaps it is, but not when that rich man is you. Do you have any idea what a pain in the ass you can be? Sometimes it would be easier to love a cactus."

His laugh was broken, and it tore her heart to hear it. "You are too much, Holly Craig. You and that smart mouth." He drew in a breath. "Please marry me. Please come home and bring our son and let me spend the rest of my life making it up to you for being so blind and stupid."

"Yes," she said simply. Because it was right. Because there was nowhere else she'd rather be than in this man's arms for the rest of her life.

His smile was filled with relief and tenderness. "Then let me do this right," he said. Before she knew what he was about, he pulled a box from his pocket and dropped to one knee. "Marry me, Holly Craig. Fill my life with light and happiness. Tease me, exasperate me, challenge me—and never give up on me."

"Do it, *signorina,*" the dark-haired woman urged.

Holly laughed. As if she could do anything else when she had the great Drago di Navarra on his knees in front of her. As if she wanted to.

"It's a deal," she said softly. "No contract required."

Drago slipped the ring on her finger. Then he got to his feet and kissed her right there in the middle of the train as everyone cheered.

EPILOGUE

DRAGO LOOKED UP from the photos he'd been studying and found his wife standing in his office, looking amazingly gorgeous in a simple dress and flats.

"I didn't hear you come in," he said.

"Obviously." She came and looked over his shoulder. And then she sighed. "Are you sure about these?"

"Of course. You are the most gorgeous model to ever grace a fragrance ad."

"I think your colleagues are going to think you've lost your mind," she grumbled.

He turned and put his hands on her waist. "Holly, you are precisely what I wanted for this campaign. You're gorgeous but approachable. Women will buy this perfume in droves."

She ran her hands through his hair. And then she kissed him. "I think they'll buy Colette in greater droves."

He laughed. "You could be right. I guess we'll see when we launch it in the spring, yes?"

She arranged herself on his lap. He did not mind. His arms went around her and held her tight. How had he ever, *ever* thought he could live without her?

"I'm perfectly confident," she said. And then she frowned. "But, Drago, I'm afraid I can't work in your fragrance development lab as first planned."

He studied her face, shocked at this news. "But you

insisted you wanted this. You've proved to me how good you are, and I've been counting on adding your expertise to the staff."

She toyed with the lapel of his collar. "Yes, well, you can still have that expertise. But I'm afraid the scents will be too much for me. In a lab. At home, I can do it when I'm feeling well. But all those scents? No, not happening."

Drago shook his head. She'd left him about a mile back, standing on the side of the road and staring at her dust cloud. "I'm not following you," he told her.

She leaned down and kissed his nose. "Oh, you darling man. No, I suppose it wouldn't make a lick of sense to you. The smells, my darling, will be too much for a woman in my condition."

He felt as if his brain was stuck in the mud, spinning tires—

And then he came unstuck and her meaning dawned. "You're pregnant?"

Her smile could have lit up the grid. "Yes."

Drago squeezed her tight, unable to say a word. And then he panicked and let her go again. "I'm sorry, was that too much?"

"No, of course not." She squeezed him back and they sat together, holding each other and laughing.

"I almost forgot," he said. He pulled open a drawer and took out some papers. "I just got these. I wanted to surprise you."

Holly took the papers and opened them. Tears filled her lovely blue eyes as she read the deed. "Gran's house."

"Your house," he said, the lump in his throat nearly too big to get the words past.

"*Our* house," she said, squeezing him tight. "Oh, Drago, thank you."

He pushed her hair back from her face, tucking it behind her ears. And then he drew her down and kissed her sweetly. "Anything for you, Holly. Anything."

She made his life complete. Her and Nicky. And this new baby, whoever he or she turned out to be. Drago's heart was full as he kissed her again. Life was full.

And it always would be. In that, he had complete faith.

* * * * *

Merry Christmas

& A Happy New Year!

Thank you for a wonderful
2013...

Come in from the cold this Christmas with two of
our favourite authors. Whether you're jetting off to
Vermont with Sarah Morgan or settling down for
Christmas dinner with Fiona Harper, the smiles
won't stop this festive season.

Visit:
www.millsandboon.co.uk

MB452

Join the Mills & Boon Book Club

Want to read more **Modern**™ books?
We're offering you **2 more** absolutely **FREE!**

We'll also treat you to these fabulous extras:

- 🌹 **Exclusive offers and much more!**
- 🌹 **FREE home delivery**
- 🌹 **FREE books and gifts with our special rewards scheme**

Get your free books now!

visit www.millsandboon.co.uk/bookclub
or call Customer Relations on 020 8288 2888

FREE BOOK OFFER TERMS & CONDITIONS